The Local Stranger

by

James Calemine

Valdosta, Georgia 31601
Printed and bound in the United States of America
Copyright © James Calemine 2019
Photograph by James Calemine
All Rights Reserved
ISBN: 978-0-9979353-5-6

No part of this book may be used or reproduced in any manner for the purpose of ... to take necessary or by non-credit educational any ... are given a forum ...

Snake~Nation~Press
Valdosta, Georgia 2019

Snake Nation Press, the only independent literary press in south Georgia, publishes *Snake Nation Review*, a book of poetry by a single author each year, and a book of fiction by a single author each year. Unsolicited submissions of fiction, essays, art, and poetry are welcome throughout the year but will not be returned unless a stamped, self-addressed envelope is included. We encourage simultaneous submissions.

Published by Snake Nation Press
110 West Force Street
Valdosta, Georgia 31601
Printed and bound in the United States of America.
Copyright © James Calemine2018
Photography by James Calemine
All Rights Reserved
ISBN: 978-0-9979353-5-6

Table of Contents

Foreword

I first heard tell of James Calemine when my band was playing a little club in Valdosta, Georgia, back in the early '90s. Griffin Bufkin was behind the bar; he was the one who had booked us to play, and he was the bartender that early evening. He served up the beers and liquor drinks, and then he played a cassette that proved to be a Bob Dylan mix tape. I've always been a huge Dylan fan, so this seemed a good omen for the night. Then a certain song played that I'd never heard before: it was "God Knows" from the *Under the Red Sky* album, I found out later. But at the time I was baffled I hadn't heard the song before...usually, nobody knew more about Dylan than I did. I asked Griffin: "Hey man, who made this tape?"

"A guy named James Calemine."

Alright. I knew I had to meet this guy, sooner or later...and a few months down the line I did, in the Roadhouse, a downtown bar in Athens, Georgia...James and Griffin were in there drinking, and I happened to wander in, and Griffin introduced us...and I knew right away that James and I were blood brothers, compadres, kindred spirits, whatever you wanta call it...and a few brief months later, we were roommates. James and I and Eric Carter, sharing a small apartment on Grady Avenue in Athens. Eric and I had the two bedrooms, and James set up his bed in the living room area. It was meant to be. We were, if such things are possible, mystically preordained to spend all that time together, drink all that moonshine together, get in all that trouble together.

These kinds of things are hard to explain, but occasionally you meet someone you almost recognize even though they're a stranger. That was the deal with James and me, and Eric too...Eric and I played in a band called Bloodkin, and though other musicians came and went through our lineup, it was James who really seemed like a third member of the band. He knew some of the songs better than the other musicians ever did, He would hear me working on the songs: I'd be in my room playing acoutic guitar, droning a riff over and over and inprovising lyrics, while James would be in kitchen area, clickety-klacking away on his typewriter...and by the time I would finish a song, he'd have it memorized. It felt righteous, living with two brotherly artists...it felt like our own private version of the Beat Generation. We had different mediums, approaces, styles, but shared a feverish dedication to our Art and Fun. James and I would each write our version of life events we saw happening around us; separate depictions that confirmed one another. And Eric's guitar playing wove the soundtrack of our stories, the feel, the mood. We were wild boys, alright—stoned, sloppy and prolific—it was an epic season of our youth, those early days in the apartment.

I remember one evening at our kitchen table, James and I started discussing William Burroughs' famous quote about Kerouac: "Well, Kerouac was a writer. That is he wrote. And many people who call themselves writers and have their names on book jackets are not writers and they can't write. The difference being a bullfighter who fights bulla bull is different to a bullshiter who makes passes with no bull there,"

And James lived up to that definition of a writer. He sat at that kitchen table, pounding away on his typewriter for hours and hours, almost every night. "That is he wrote." I knew a lot of other people at the time who claimed to be writers, but who always seemed to be out in the bars drinking, bragging, glorifying...while James was always back home, working and working. He also kept a camera with him at all times, and was as determined about keeping a photographic record as he was about his writing. His work ethic was a clear lesson, and one of the early reasons I knew James was the real deal.

But James always repeated a mantra to us: "This ain't gonna last." He always warned us to appreciate it while we had it, our crazed little artistic gang...he seemed to view the whole situation from a higher vantage point, a novelist's longterm grasp of our storyline...but life sneaks on by, of course, and as James predicted, nowadays that apartment seems like ancient history. But what remains is the work.

And here we have it. A fine selection of James' work; some written back in the good old apartment days, some newer. I've just started reading through the stories in this book, and the first one is "Money and Snakes"...and my initial impression is, it's like a lyrical mirror image of the early scene in Flannery O'Connor's *Wise Blood,* where Hazel Motes tells the lady across from him on the train, "I reckon you think you been redeemed".....but "Money and Snakes" is short and symbolic, a little dream song that paints a vivid portrait, mysterious and gorgeous.

The Local Stranger

One of my favorite pieces of James' has always been "The Local Stranger"...I first read it back on Grady Avenue in the early '90s, and it struck a bittersweet note that lingered with me for days, the kind of peculiar atmosphere so few artists are able to create. I knew when I first read this story what a strange, cool voice James possesses: Southern, romantic, haunted, red clay rustic and switchblade vicious by turns.

And another thing, now, again, reading through these stories James has sent me, I'm reminded that he's one of the few people I've ever known that I could truly talk to about the Bible, religion, etc....he always approached these subjects with reverence but not blind obedience, and he could always write passages that renewed my faith, without sounding the least bit preachy, which is about as much as you can ask from a piece of art. How many writers could depict spirituality in terms so strong and simple as "O Street Baptist Church"...? In fact, what do we even call this piece of writing? I don't think it's exactly a short story...maybe an essay in the tradition of E.B. White? Maybe a little freeform gospel song? It's certainly not inappropriate to describe James Calemine as a rare poet, even when he's working in prose...but ultimately the categories don't matter. All that matters are the words themselves, and James' words are high octane, electric, significant. He isn't "famous" yet, but that's a whole different ball game. I'll go ahead and say it: He's one of our great living American writers, and that's a sure bet. To quote Thelonious Monk: "I say play your own way. Don't play what the public wants. Play what you want and let the public pick up on what you are doing, even if it takes them fifteen or twenty years."

Yep. They'll pick up on Jimmy eventually, but meanwhile those of us who discovered him early can claim a kind of kinship...we arrived at the show before the dance floor got too crowded. We're lucky.

Daniel Hutchens
Athens, GA

Reviews

"James Calemine's heart and writing justify him being respected by anybody." --Stanley Booth
Author of The True Adventures of the Rolling Stones, Rythm Oil, Keith: Til' I Roll Over Dead and Red, Hot and Blue.

"James Calemine's writing executes a perfect balance of soul to science, flourish to frankness, and imagery to movement. His writing reveals awareness of the intricacies of life--the human experience--with a "lifted" perspective." --Eleanor Underhill, Underhill Rose

"It's certainly not inappropriate to describe James Calemine as a rare poet, even when he's working in prose...but ultimately the categories don't matter. All that matters are the words themselves, and James' words are high octane, electric, significant. I'll go ahead and say it: He's one of our great living American writers, and that's a sure bet." --Daniel Hutchens, Bloodkin

"James Calemine is one of my favorite writers." --Todd Nance, Widespread Panic, Interstellar Boys.

"Imagine walking down a dirt road in rural south Georgia. A chorus of cicadas, crickets, banjos and frogs permeate the air. It's dusk and your mind is soaring on poetic thermals! A southern gothic daydream! Snake nation! Spanish moss! It all makes sense now..." --Mark Neill, Grammy-winning producer.

"James Calemine is a seeker of truth...which makes him a good friend of mine." --Marc Ford, The Black Crowes, Ben Harper & The Magpie Salute.

"James Calemine. That's a good name. I'll remember that name." --Harry Crews, Author of Florida Frenzy, Feast of Snakes, The Gospel Singer and others.

Money And Snakes

"Everyone has a vice. The world is constructed upon vice," the silver-haired gentleman stated as he exhaled pungent blue smoke from his nostrils. He spoke to a young man sitting across from him in the train cabin.

"You spoke of irony...the world's immensities are revealed in a day especially in this voyeuristic American society. History awaits specific actions to transpire."

The silver-haired gentleman smilcd. A sinister chill lingered in his wisdom. He smoked again from his pipe. "Everything is ironic in a biblical sense. Or, at least coincidentally symbolic."

The listening passenger turned his gaze from the distinguished stranger, and looked past his own reflection in the window toward unfamiliar landscape. He grew tired of talk and stale smoke.

"These are dangerously symbolic times. Many telling events await to fulfill sealed prophecies. You, my traveling friend, possess such a sharp insight."

"What insight?" the young passenger asked, somewhat confused and fascinated by the stranger's hypnotic voice.

"The realization that all your transgressions will return and make you accountable for everything you've done in your life." The distinguished stranger knocked ash out of his pipe into a glass ashtray as he observed the young traveler avoiding his gaze by staring out at the vast desert landscape passing by. The stranger then said: "Just as everything morphs into its opposite. You understand ironic vice infects a soul's pureness. Seeds of any downfall is vice."

A blood-red sunset awoke the young passenger as the train jerked to a stop. The silver-haired stranger was gone. Six o'clock. Arrival time. He rubbed his eyes as he looked out the window and noticed fellow travelers holding and pulling luggage as they waited for the vehicle to transport them to their destination.

Like a dream, his black-haired maiden appeared in the crowd. She was waiting for him with a beautiful patience. He smiled, knowing salvation was close at hand.

The Local Stranger

The first day Jake noticed Dex Metlock was a blistering hot Fourth of July afternoon. A white heat evoked shimmering mirages along the restless coast. A humid mist floated above the shore. The tide was rising. Festive sunbathers were forced to move their belongings as the dark waters pushed them closer to the sand dunes.

A dense shoreline crowd made for tight quarters under the sun. The sky was not a deep azure, but a light china blue caused from still air and intense heat. From the shore, it looked as if the shrimp boats off the coast, dragging their nets, were only huge toys dangling near the horizon.

Dex Metlock was wearing a red bandana around his head. He wore cutoffs, faded and frayed blue jeans. His beard looked near three weeks old. His India ink tattoos were visible, but indistinct from a distance. Dex's skin looked like tanned leather.

He was drinking from a nearly empty bottle of Jim Beam. Dex brought attention to the floating ant at the bottom of the bottle. The festivity gripped his mind. He carried on as if he were a member of some obscure jubilee.

"Red liquor! Fever fire!"

Dex was singing loud and out of tune with a ponytailed kid playing an acoustic guitar. Dex was sitting on a beer cooler. Several of his teeth were missing. He looked like a deranged pirate, or a drunken carpenter. Cosmic waves of activity electrified the festive Fourth of July shore. The scene was a panoramic montage of an all-American holiday.

After several hours of reckless drinking, Dex passed out, face down in the sand. The rising tide splashed an incoming wave on his leg, and would have carried him out to sea had he not come to his senses.

According to stories told by locals, Dex was an insane drunk. He was a native of the seaside community, yet no one knew the facts of his life for the last fifteen years. For the past two summers, Dex returned to his hometown shores. Dex slept in the sand dunes. He rested in the public shower house during adverse weather conditions.

All sorts of exaggerated stories surfaced and circulated in local cliques. Often when describing Dex to someone, locals often remarked, "Oh, yeah, the bum, I know who you're talking about," with dim recollections of someone they never met.

One story claimed Dex escaped from a mental institution. Another story went as far as to say he killed his girlfriend while other rumors claimed he was a rapist, a circus freak, a bank robber, a Satanist.

Many locals were sure Dex was a crazy local nuisance. Most of the recreational crowds were not excited about a homeless derelict living several hundred feet from where their daughters and wives lie asleep in the sun wearing scant bikinis. Many of the wealthiest community members bathed in the sun and water farther up the beach near private land owned by a country club.

Wealthy locals hold no affinity for homegrown prophets or homeless artists; such people are too concerned with ignoring tolerance and assassinating the individual's character. None of the locals could fathom Dex originating an unpatented game that could entertain thousands. The vulgar mob doesn't look at anything too close, until it's too late.

On this Fourth of July afternoon, Jake would only notice a surface reaction and common contempt Dex conjured among various cliques and individuals. Ironic time would present future dimensions of closer exposure toward these unknown faces in seasons unborn.

The next week, Jake left town for an employment opportunity. For almost a year, he forgot about Dex Metlock.

April blue skies shined a seasonal color as sights and scents bloomed while winter was forgotten. Jake lounged in the sand dunes with two girlfriends. He was watching Lindsay, a beautiful brunette, apply pure olive oil to her long legs to intensify the tanning process.

Her black two-piece bikini amplified her already tan body. Anna, the natural blonde, was asleep in her leopard-skin bikini, on a fold-out plastic beach chair. She breathed deep breaths of calmness.

The breeze was still cool. The sand dunes blocked the chilly ocean breeze. The sun was pleasant if one could hide from the wind. A new scent of the season evoked memories of something forgotten in the past.

"Jake, have you made our reservations at Dixie's Bait Shack for Friday?"

"Not yet, Lindsay."

"Seems to me you shouldn't have to make reservations considering all the time you've worked there."

"I'll tell Tony this afternoon."

Jake noticed a fellow walking toward them from the shell-paved beach entrance. He tried to duck down and stay obscured by the camphor weeds and sea oats, but it appeared the man already spotted them.

It only took Jake a moment to remember this approaching stranger was the local homeless fellow, Dex Metlock. Jake was aware of the man's reputation and was prepared for any obnoxious scene. What a lure, he thought, a cooler full of beer and two beautiful girls.

Jake turned his gaze away from the stranger toward the horizon. He took another drink of beer. The ocean breeze was brisk. Nearby, someone was applying coconut oil and the scent drifted back toward the dunes. Gray and white seagulls squawked and gathered in troupes on the calm shoreline.

It was Tuesday. Most people were at work. Summer crowds were not yet in force. This was Jake's favorite time of year. He looked back toward the entrance, and a more vivid image was before him than his last memory of Dex, the previous Fourth of July, with his face down in the sand.

"Girls, I believe we have a visitor."

When Dex approached with a ornery look in his eyes, he was barefoot. His tan faded the primitive dragon tattoo covering his left shoulder and arm. A spider web spawned across his chest. Dex's matted brown hair was cut short around his neck and ears, but long enough to reach his eyebrows. His physique was slender and taut, giving no indication of his homeless condition, aside from his unwashed jean shorts.

"Excuse me. My name is Dex. It's really Dexter, but please call me Dex. Sorry to intrude, but may I be so bold as to ask if y'all could spare an old boy a beer?"

"Sure." Jake pulled a Coors can out of the cooler, knocked off the ice, and handed it to Dex, who grinned an incisor-voided smile. He wore a full beard.

"I appreciate it very much. By the way, what are your names?"

"This is Lindsay, and this is Anna." A slight bow from Dex.

"Ladies. And what is your name, kind sir?" "Jake." They shook hands.

"It is a pleasure to meet such beautiful, enlightened young people. I will not forget the beverage gesture. I'll be on my way. Thank you very much."

Dex bowed again and walked a few hundred feet down the beach and sat down in a rusted beach chair he was carrying. Jake sensed no harm from Dex's demeanor.

Jake was scheduled to work at Dixie's this evening. Most of his days were spent on the beach or fishing with friends before he was off to work at night, shucking oysters and tapping kegs of beer. The year before, Jake was arrested for public drunkenness and eluding a police officer, tarnishing his name within local elites and friends' families. He was labeled a troublemaker.

Jake watched Dex get out of his chair to assist a pregnant woman in setting up her umbrella while her other child distracted her. The mother was so grateful for help she noticed nothing out of the ordinary about Dex.

...

That spring and summer, a familiar crowd gathered day after day at Sumner's Point. The Point, as locals called it, was a section of the beach located very close to the Mossy Oaks Hotel, a four-star resort. Dex was at the beach every day. He appeared from behind the sand dunes in the morning, grimacing in the damaging glare of the sun.

Dex always spoke to Jake and his crowd of friends, especially Lindsay and Anna, though he never came on to either of the girls. Some days, he asked Jake for a beer. Other days, Jake would give him a couple beers to stimulate conversation. Regardless, he always made a brief appearance to speak to Jake.

...

It was a quiet breezy Wednesday in May with not a cloud in the sky. On this day, Jake learned of the game. After the first beer of the afternoon was opened Dex tossed a golf ball to Jake.

"Jakey, walk eleven paces away from where I am standing, and dig a golfball-size hole in the sand."

Dex demonstrated by digging his hole first. Three inches deep. Dex built up a ramp of sand behind the hole.

The object was to stand behind one's own hole as a boundary, and attempt to roll the golf ball into the opponent's hole.

Making the shot would depend on the day's sandbank. The coastline was eroding, and the beach break was different daily according to the tide. With no predictions of the tide, a player could only become accustomed to the shifting shoreline throughout the progression of the game. The first player to score three times won.

Under nostalgic patterns of sky, beach golf seemed familiar and facile to Jake, but growing up on these shores he never saw anyone playing the game before. Jake inquired about where Dex picked it up, as he rolled preliminary warm up shots, and Dex replied:

"As far as I know, I originated it, but I'm sure somewhere else, someone will say they invented it, after they see it played."

"I've never seen anyone playing the game and I've lived here all my twenty years."

"Neither have I in all my thirty-five years. My idea would be to patent flags and distances concerning playoffs and degrees of difficulty. Perhaps even introducing a club. Hell, I'd be able to afford one of these beach houses if I could patent the idea."

Beer after beer, hour after hour, day after day, Dex and Jake played beach golf, oblivious to all that was going on around them. They didn't play on weekends because too many people had never seen such a sport, and they all wanted to play the game themselves, only bothering the players and disrupting the flow of the game. After some months, the shoreline regulars were accustomed to the game and no longer asked questions or watched.

…

In hours spent whiling away time with the game, Jake inquired about Dex's youth. The only time they saw each other was at the beach. The foundation of the friendship was built upon beach golf.

Dex admitted his life was not what it used to be. He was a carpenter by trade. He mentioned a hopeful childhood and an institution visit, but he did not elaborate on the nature or duration of his stay.

Jake discovered from his old football coach that Dex was a heavily recruited halfback. He wondered what kept Dex from following through on his talents. What went wrong? What brought him to this point?

"I hear tell you were a mean halfback in high school."

"Yeah, but I liked defense better. When I tackled people, I didn't want them to get up. Faded glory."

Overall, they did not discuss details of their personal lives. They concentrated on matters at hand. There was no regard for any other period of time other than the present moment. Such was the nature of the friendship. Money had no bearing on anything. Neither man had anything to hide. They only wanted to concentrate on the game.

...

However, the more Dex drank, the less the game interested him. When he reached a high degree of inebriation, Dex moved through the shoreline crowd, talking, asking for beer or cigarettes.

Since he slept in the sand dunes or the public shower house, the local police were aware of Dex's circumstances. When he leaned into the patrol car conversing with officers who patrolled the beach parking lot daily, he acted as if he shared a secret with them. The police did not consider Dex a menace.

Dex was an articulate conversationalist; his intelligence was obvious. Yet, no one understood why he was homeless.

Only when he would become a blind, sloppy drunk would Dex ever ask for food. On occasion, folks brought Dex something to eat from the beach concession stands such as a hamburger or hotdog; every blue moon, he was given money. If drinking all day and someone refused to give him any food, he was liable to shout vicious obscenities like, "Stingy motherfuckers. You're all a bunch of fucking hypocrites! Sheep! The wrath is gonna fall on you all without warning!"

Often while drunk, Dex struck up conversations with total strangers only to argue with an intense belligerence concerning an unrelated issue to the conversation. There were times his words would invite a serious physical beating unless someone would drag him off or subdue him. On various occasions the police were called.

...

It was early June, and Dex had not been involved in any confrontations for the past couple of months, but his freeloading, insane drunken reputation followed him no matter what state of mind or action he was in. Dex had no time to explain circumstances that brought him down this road, knowing not only that these people could never endure what he had, but also that they did not care.

Quiet mornings on the beach distill clarity to the senses. A serenity fills the bones. Time's complexity overwhelms at the shore. If the sky and ocean fail to tranquilize or wash away all problems within the mind, they boil life down to a few essential elements.

By late June, one had to run across the hot, soft sand toward the water. The feet would burn. One would also have to avoid sandspurs stabbing the feet with unexpected pain when walking or running down the beach or upon a path from the dunes.

On this humid Friday, Jake noticed Dex had already dug the holes. He was practicing at ten o'clock in the morning. Grilled barbecue could be smelled from the pit back toward the concession stand.

"Let's hit it, Jakey. You mind if I grab a beer?"

"Be my guest."

A festive vibration gathered in anticipation of a weekend party. A fanfare of motley seasiders: surfers, businessmen, sunbathers, housewives, sports freaks, bicyclers, runners, or anyone quitting work to gather at the shoreline for fun.

"Beautiful day for our festivities, Jakey."

"Let's get it on."

"You've been on a winning streak this week. I may have come up with this game, but I'll be damned if you ain't a better player."

"I'm gonna keep it goin' today."

They began to play the game. Four guys came down from the parking lot to the beach carrying coolers, footballs and horseshoes; with intense scrutiny they watched Jake and Dex play beach golf.

"I hope those rednecks stay out of our way."

"Just do your thing."

"I will if they quit gawking like idiots."

"I gotta tell you, Jakey, you're straight on the mark. I wish I could stick around and see what you're gonna come up with. I'm sure it'll be undeniable." Dex laughed.

"What the hell are you rambling about? Are you trying to get rid of me? Do you know the score is two to zero?"

"I ain't gonna be around much longer."

"Tired of takin' ass whippin's at beach golf?"

"I mean, next summer I won't be here."

"You'll be around. And spare me the flattery, because I'm one up on you." Jake took another swallow of beer. He squinted in the sun as the rising tide flooded the game.

...

One afternoon during an intermission in one of the games, Dex's friend Shelly made an appearance at the beach. Shelly was a tall, skinny peroxide blonde, who chainsmoked Marlboro reds.

Shelly brought Dex various necessities like a toothbrush, toothpaste, cigarettes, matchboxes, soap, old shirts, shorts, sandals, hats, combs and old towels. Dex never clarified his relationship with Shelly, yet it appeared they had known each other for years. Jake never asked questions.

Usually when Dex was given gifts, he was unsuspecting and very grateful. He never made anyone feel as if they had to give him anything. A few people looked out for him, but most were impervious to his charm.

...

The local public beach on the Fourth of July takes on a circuslike atmosphere. The beach becomes an over population of natives, tourists, children, dogs, fishermen, bikers, mothers, fathers, rednecks, surfers, boiledpeanut eaters, punks, barbecue junkies, smokers, drunks, police, Sunday fools, stoners and everyone and their brother who can make it to the beach on Independence Day.

Today marked the one-year anniversary of the first time Jake ever laid eyes on Dex Metlock. No mist hung over the breezeless ocean.

Dex began drinking around nine in the morning; he started consuming vodka and Gatorade with two big women sitting on their crazy faded quilts. He ate some of their potato salad. He talked romance in the bright morning light. Later in the holiday festivities, Dex continued drinking and giving away his Busch beer, from a twelve pack he managed to buy.

Dex reminded Jake of a standup comic when he was merely tipsy; his mood lightened and he became funny. He had an actor's sense of presence.

Dex was blind drunk by noon. This increase in drinking would unveil a lonely darkness hidden within depths of his frustrated sorrow. His levels of inhibition decreased. His shame faded in crowds. He believed himself to be less visible when drunk.

Dex began playing Frisbee with some locals, carrying on with drunken animation, and while chasing a free-floating disc, he crashed into a picnic table littered with middle-aged tourists. After scattering food, drinks and lunch supplies, Dex grabbed some chicken and several pieces of bread from the hot sand. Dex stumbled back to the camp with two biscuits and a chicken breast using the Frisbee as if it were a plate. He lost himself in the festiveness like the party was in his own backyard.

Radios blared along the shoreline-assorted songs sharing local stations, promoting an identical frequency lot that created a unified song of ongoing currencies echoing together as one walked down the beach. A light breeze soothed, allowing one to forget, only for a moment, how hot it becomes on the Fourth of July. Obscure scents of coconut oil, iodine, beer, sweat, marijuana and grilled food pre-served a time span——evoking memories through sensory texture.

Just after two o'clock in the afternoon, returning from a blue smoke ritual in the salt cedar and marsh elder forest with Lindsay, Jake noticed Dex was alone near the water, going through his tae kwon do motions. His isolation was an indicating level of his inebriation. Two weeks earlier, Dex lost two teeth in a fight, and received a dangerous beating initiated by him speaking with the wrong woman.

Jake sat down with his friends. He opened a beer. What a holiday. No one went to work today. He loved long weekends.

"There goes Dex," said one of Jake's friends in a voice of re-signed acceptance.

Jake was feeling festive and curious; he walked down toward the water to see what the sudden commotion was about. A small crowd gathered. Jake was looking toward the lifeguard stand, and in full view of everyone, Dex began running up and down the shoreline, screaming, pointing at the sky, like he spotted something in the air.

Dex acted as if he were loading a bazooka or mortar, with a tar-get in sight. Dex fired at an invisible vessel in the sky. He made the sound effect of two explosions and watched the invisible vessel fall from the abyss, into the ocean.

Dex let out a war cry, raising his arms in victory, and then walked back through an astonished crowd to his rusted beach chair in the sand dunes, where he lay down and passed out as if nothing happened.

Jake witnessed people with their mouths open in astonishment, unsure of what they'd just seen. Others shook their heads; some laughed, antagonized, pointed, jested, "You idiot, get a fucking job. Go sleep in the garbage." No one understood the intended humor of Dex's performance.

Jake could not take his bloodshot eyes from the red, white and blue Budweiser hat floating in the foam of the rising tide near Dex. After the performance, Jake walked to the edge of the dunes where Dex was resting and tried to talk to him, but Dex was blind and incoherent. He recognized Jake and slurred in a whiskey laced voice: "Great day for an American Jakey," and then Dex began to snore.

The Fourth of July was a typical stunt Dex performed to keep people guessing as well as contributing to the public's notions of his mental instability. Yet, no one witnessed Dex's maddening evenings under the stars, praying to God to allow him to find a way out of such forsaken circumstances. The local vultures never weighed the odds, tragedy or tribulation stacked against the man; underneath Dex's mask of random insanity and reckless drunkenness, was a lonely, intelligent guy down on his luck and conditions of life.

...

As summer rolled on, Dex was more subdued at the beach. His appearances were not as predictable. When he did appear at the beach, he began wading out in the ocean.

With his feet, Dex unearthed sand dollars embedded a few feet in the thick underwater sand. In the evenings, he would bleach the sand dollars he found that day, and allow them to dry on newspapers he laid out under the stars near his night time fire in the dunes.

After drying the sand dollars, Dex painted a light sheer gloss on them. Once dry, he painted zen-like symbols and cryptic characters to sell to yankee tourists for three dollars apiece. Open hearted locals bought sand dollars from Dex for one dollar. His trade made possible by Shelly's kind gift of supplies rendered the locals more tolerant toward him.

...

The summer burned away. Coastal communities learn from seasonal wisdoms of the past. The economy slows down. September reminded the coastal community it was hurricane season. Summer was over. Jake had fewer friends who would accompany him to the beach to play golf, drink, talk, swim or waste time. He knew these days were fading fast.

Warnings of a tropical storm were in the news. In just a day or so, the storm was to be on Sumner's Point. Huge cottonball-shaped clouds floated just off the shore. The clouds were not pure white, but black and ominous, like smoke from an oil fire. The storm was approaching.

Jake knew the season was over. He began to feel foolish at the beach during this time of year. A season had passed. He wanted to see Dex one last time for the year.

Jake sat alone on the shore. The few people who were at the beach were beginning to leave. The storm served as a reminder for the dangerous chance hurricane season delivers. As he opened a newspaper, he heard someone call his name.

"Jakey! I knew you'd be here!" Dex strolled down the beach with a brown paper bag under each arm. "Damn, son, where you been?"

"Seasons are changing, Jakey. You can't fight change. Something here I want you to see. But drink a beer first."

Dex opened up one of the paper bags and handed Jake a beer. He opened the other paper bag and spread out almost twenty painted sand dollars on a beach towel.

"Did these with watercolors." Dex pointed to a few lightcolored painted sand dollars with esoteric signs and obscure symbols. Jake inspected a black and red painted sand dollar.

"Looking at the Chinese Kite," said Dex, "that's one of my favorites. You can keep that one. But take all you want. Even though I know you ain't the sand dollar type."

"That's fine. I'll just keep this one. Sell the rest."

"I haven't made much money, only enough to buy supplies, keep a bottle in the dunes, and buy a hot dog here and there. But the others weren't watercolors. I should've painted these earlier in the season."

The beach was empty. The kids were back in school. September hurricane warnings warded off sunbathers. No radio could be heard. The distant blanket of storm clouds moved closer from the horizon to the shoreline.

"You wanna play one?"

"I forgot a ball. I'm gonna go to the pier and see if I can sell any of these, even though the season is dead. We'll play tomorrow."

The following day, the threatening storm had not passed. The beach was desolate. Even gulls were unseen. Winds from the south were gaining strength. Jake felt he was becoming shiftless and pestilent abiding by the same routine. He decided no matter if Dex showed or not, this would be his last day at the beach until next spring. Jake remembered Dex saying he was unsure concerning his winter home. Dex hated the cold. He claimed he spent all of his winters in Florida.

There was a strange sky hovering over the beach. It seemed everything was under a dome of lead. Jake felt things would never be the same after today, as if this era in his life would be forever disconnected from his self and immediate circumstances, surroundings, friendships and employment would all morph into some faded memory.

As Jake drove into the parking lot, he noticed Dex speaking with three men. Dex was speaking with animated fervor. The three men were all tattooed and drinking. They did not seem to appreciate what Dex was telling them. Jake parked away from the public shower house in the corner of the empty parking lot. He did not take off his shoes, shirt or hat.

He carried a towel as he walked down the familiar shelled path toward the beach. The wind was constant. The tide rose as if some unforeseen force pushed the waters higher on the shore. A sea mist floated above the waters.

Jake looked over his shoulder, back up the path, and he noticed Dex following him, walking towards the beach with his head down. Dex was carrying a brand new lawn chair. He was wearing a red Hawaiian shirt, a golf hat, sunglasses and a pair of tan shorts. He carried a brown paper bag under his left arm. He looked respectable.

Jake knew it was a strange time of year for new seaside paraphernalia. Despite the cosmetic change, Dex appeared melancholy. Sober, even.

Once they got down to the shore, they noticed the battalions of storm clouds that filled the sky and marched toward them. Dex pulled a golf ball out of his side pocket on the new khaki shorts.

"Looks like we don't have much time to declare a champion," said Dex. "Only one warmup shot apiece."

"Looks like the last game of the year."

"The last one forever, Jake."

Jake offered no remark concerning the gravity of Dex's utterance. They began digging the golf holes. It was obvious Dex was tired and distracted while setting up camp.

"Let's play the seven-foot overtime deck."

Jake attempted to make the game interesting by moving the holes four paces closer, making it easier to score. Once Dex stopped digging, he sat down in the sand. He reached for his beer. He looked at the sky.

"A lot more goes on than the poor human eye sees. Y'know all this is an illusion, right?"

"There are arguments for that."

"This test called life is a strange thing. There is more to it than what our senses tell us. We can hear and touch, taste, smell and see everything, but there is something else watching and allowing coincidences and ironies to occur, and it's called God. So, all these worries and concerns people have, about what people think of them, or who dies with the most money, or who is more famous. To me, the truest of the true are the ones who suffer and strive for others... not the rich. Life is worth more than fitting a profile of a wealthy television image."

Dex drained the last of his beer. He did not stand. He pulled out two more cans of Budweiser from the paper bag. He put the bag back under the brand-new lawn chair still smelling of fresh plastic, and handed a beer to Jake, who began to have second thoughts about Dex's sobriety.

The dark pillows of clouds seemed to blot out all sounds. A calm before the storm. Dex looked toward the sky as if some explanation for his dilemmas were somewhere within the dark density of the clouds. There were no signs of summer in the sky.

"I was fired in Tampa because I watched a little girl's dog get run over by a car and when I went down to console her and help out, they accused me of leaving the job site without permission. So they fired me.

"I've always been the odd man out. Never had rich parents. I had no inheritance to live off of like a lot of these idiots; to them it has nothing to do with earning money, or the desolation of misfortune. Many wealthy people believe poor people are stupid. I've always carried around this faith that being poor, especially if you try not to be, is okay. For me, it's the opposite of an inborn fear.

"The rich never understand the difference money makes. They claim it brings on more problems, but the problems are not as serious as the ones that come from having no money. Those with life-long wealth will never understand this concept. You're either blessed or cursed to know this, I can't decide, but I don't complain and yet, I'd like to see some of these candy asses walk a mile in my moccasins. Only God knows the story. He is the only judge.

"Money doesn't fool me. These people are no better than me because they have deep bank accounts, but you can't explain this to them; they'll hate you; they'll snuff you out if they have a chance. Those motherfuckers don't care, Jakey. Listen to me, you're young, and idealistic, but things are gonna get harder. Money brings a better life. But it does not make the life.

"I know I'm not wrong. But what a terrible price to pay for being right. Yet, in spite of this insight, Jakey, I've managed to piss everything away. Pissed away all my talent and all my leverage.

"Now here I am on this dreary beach, drinking this shit, losing my mind. I have nothing. It's a terrible view I'm looking from. The only thing I have to look forward to is you coming down and playing beach golf with me, Jakey. You've got soul, Jake. I've always said that. You know I invented that fucking game."

"You should patent the game."

"Patent the game? You know how much money that takes? It's not easy to patent something, especially when you sleep on the beach and keep all of your belongings in a plastic trash bag. There is too much legwork for a homeless man to patent anything. It's twisted justice, and things don't seem to be getting any better."

The low black clouds looked evil and dangerous. Dex watched an ant wandering to a small hole in the sand while a regiment of others, marching in a singlefile line, with an unrelated intention and destination, scaled the vast desert beyond, toward home. Dex handed Jake another beer.

"It's a cold, heartless world. I know it may sound selfish, but you've got to live for yourself amid everyday bullshit tribulations. There won't be anything left of you, if you don't. I'm not saying do not love thy neighbor, love them but don't try and save their soul. You can't do that. The only power you have is to save your own soul, and if you do that in accordance with God, you won't be just living for yourself. It's easy to be a hypocrite and pass judgement on others. Some people don't know how hard it's gonna get for them.

"Bank accounts of the damned. They judge and hate so easily. I'm not talking about working people; they are too busy surviving, paying the bills. But no matter how much pain and sorrow your faith may cause you, you can't betray instinct, even if it kills you. If you do, you'll run the risk of being one of these hypocrites, who are all so vain, believing their opinions make them talented and worth gold.

"Those vultures are just wasting away operating on illusion, believing their opinions will last forever. It's an evil world. Shit, man, even when you have faith, they'll crucify you."

Dex let out a long sigh. He rubbed his eyes as if to see the oncoming storm clearer. Distant thunder rumbled in the heavens.

"I think of the Bible a lot, Jake. I've had one of those small green Gideon's since high school. I often think of the passage that begins 'Oh God save me, may those who seek my life be put to shame and confusion; may all those who desire my ruin be turned back in disgrace.'"

Dex poured the last of his beer into his mouth without opening his eyes. He let out a low belch.

"I suppose I'm being punished for drinking too much despite realizing its foolishness."

They began the game. Tremendous explosions of thunder reverberated across the sky. Distant lightning spliced the horizon. Further conversation was unnecessary. Past days of shared folly on familiar shores enlightened some vague telepathy. Another flash of lightning lit up the dark noon and disappeared as if a celestial bulb had exploded. No ships could be seen on the horizon. A biblical mist covered the sea.

Visibility was low. A sense of time was untraceable. These two friends, like ghosts alone on the beach amid a dream, ignored the storm. Neither of the players wanted to walk away from this era of friendship.

Thunder exploded like an asphalt building cracking open, sending a heavenly shudder through the blood as if an echoing wisdom reminded change could not be ignored.

"This storm looks serious," said Dex, scratching his head. "It may be the blackest sky I've ever seen."

The approaching rain sounded like a cosmic drone, or some demented applause falling over the ocean. Another splice of lightning lit up the dark noon not far down the beach.

"We're like unwanted guests, Jakey."

"Let's split."

"It's a sign."

They gathered their belongings and started for the Sumner Point beach entrance. The rain was on them.

"Hell fire, boy, the bottom is gonna drop out," yelled Dex as he managed to throw away his beer cans while running by a county garbage barrel.

They were both running. Millions of godsent water bullets pounded the beach and ocean without regard for any human concern. Skeletons of rain remained in the untrodden sand. Dex ran for the shower house. Jake ran for his car.

"Take cover, Jakey!" Dex was laughing. They were running on separate paths exploding orbits. Dex was jumping over boxwood hedges toward the concrete shower house.

Once he was in his car, the windows steaming and him soaked, Jake realized he never got the chance to wish Dex good luck or adios in affirmation of their friendship. Jake always believed he would see Dex again so he didn't see a point in driving back to the public concession area.

After the last time they played golf, the rain did not stop for ten days. Local concerns surrounded the unpredictable weather hurricane fears allowing residents to forget outofseason concerns.

The winter did not descend until mid-November. Jake began inquiring through various sources on Dex's whereabouts. Vague tales claimed he murdered someone.

Someone murdered him. Other stories told of Dex selling out, becoming employed, taking prescribed medication and getting fat. However, no matter the degree of truth in the tales, Dex was not seen upon his hometown shores again. In time, he faded from the collective community's memory.

...

Years later, Jake returned to the coast for a funeral. Broke and emotionally exhausted, he wanted to sit alone at The Point and remember better days.

He sat at his favorite inlet on a wooden bench. The bench was not there when he was growing up. Small changes had transformed the place over the years. An opulent banquet hall was added to the Mossy Oaks Hotel. A receding shoreline faded into condominiums and tourist shops.

There was enough change to make him long for what it used to look like. Complex time conjured old riddles formed from crafty and foolish plans laid long ago bringing forth the fruit of those designs.

Jake noticed near the shallow low tide, two middle-aged men playing beach golf in the identical area he and Dex played years before. The ironies of his past and present overwhelmed him on his hometown shores as these two imposters carried on with their charade.

An unusually cool breeze mocked the June heat. Jake could not shake the serendipity of attending a funeral, and discovering this maddening scene. He watched the men toss the golf ball with motions of young girls unfamiliar with techniques or fundamentals of the game, or any sport.

A heavy-set man, wearing an Australian lifeguard hat, gold bracelets and a Rolex watch conducted himself with the utmost confidence. The other player, a gray-haired man with thin, pale, alcoholic legs, was lobbing the golf ball in a feeble manner. The holes were too close together.

The men appeared to be in their fifties. They were drinking what looked to be orange juice in small bar glasses. Jake noticed they were either living in or renting the large three-story beach house a few hundred feet away.

They had no sense of the game. Jake knew they could never handle Dex Metlock's marathon playoff sessions. He felt a nauseous feeling in his stomach. It was a haunting and cruel day. He watched the gimpy, rich alcoholics pretending to play beach golf for some time. He heard them compliment one another on their skills.

Jake heard the hatless man inform a curious beach walker who inquired on the nature of the sport.

"We're considering putting a patent on this game, and taking it on the road to see how far we can run with it."

Jake wanted to run down to the beach and say that they would not patent anything, that he was not there from the beginning with the originator of the game long before these charlatans discovered their act.

Jake felt a burning in his stomach. He was having difficulty breathing. It seemed a perverse joke was being played on him by some invisible jester. A fateful torment. He stood up from the initial-carved wooden bench and walked away from the beach, toward the parking lot. A smell of gardenias overwhelmed him, and he was saddened by their sweetness. He had no resources to prove Dex originated the game. A disorienting sorrow wracked his bones.

Without noticing, Jake stumbled through a row of azaleas and holly trees, scratching his arms, and walked down the Mossy Oak's colorful mosaic sidewalk leading toward the new banquet hall.

A young dark-haired waiter, smoking a cigarette, in his maroon hotel uniform, stopped Jake under a low awning and without hostility but, a firm grip on his shoulder said: "Sir, you are not a guest here. I'm afraid you'll have to return to the beach."

Jake could not bring himself to say anything to the waiter. He walked toward the exit of these expensive hotel grounds, and shuddered at his future. He walked with his head down.

When he finally looked, he noticed Anna Blackshear, his old beach pal, walking toward him with two children. Each caught the other's eye. She was alone besides the young girls. He could tell by the look in her eyes, she knew about the funeral. She'd spent many days upon these very same shores with him.

"Oh my, Jake, is that you?" They embraced as old memories flooded his mind.

"You're beautiful as ever."

"And you're just as handsome. Jake, I'm so sorry about your father. He was great. My mom told me the news."

"Are these your girls?"

"This is Ashley and this is Audrey. Say hello to Mr. Jake. He's an old friend of Mama's."

"They'll be as beautiful as you. You married? Obviously."

"Yeah. About eight years. He's at work."

"Well, I'll let you go," said Jake, as Ashley, the oldest daughter, picked a gardenia and gave it to him.

"Well, how nice."

"Let me put it in your lapel," said Anna.

"Feels like the old days," he said, looking into her dark blue eyes knowing time had eroded everything between them. They gave each other a prolonged hug.

"Those old feelings never go away, do they? Sorry about your Dad. And don't be a local stranger when you come home."

As he walked to the car, the fresh gardenia scent reminded him of funeral flowers. The past was dead...

O Street Baptist Church

A tidal shift forever altered my life. The past evaporated. A dark time hounded me. A culmination of events and circumstances tested my spirit. The job and finances just weren't cutting it, and I'd been waiting around for a deal that never seemed to arrive. I missed my daughter. Eroded bonds in a relationship transpired beyond repair. A behavioral sink seemed to permeate every move I made.

During this time, I couldn't concentrate. A couple of times, I was almost moved to tears while driving. My sadness overwhelmed. One day at work, I almost broke down, and had to leave early. An era had ended. The past still possessed a firm grip on me.

That weekend I was invited by an African-American co worker to the O Street Baptist Church. It had been awhile since I'd been to church, and I knew it couldn't hurt anything. It would be good for me. I was the only Caucasian to attend. Upon entering the small church, I noticed a bass player, drummer, guitarist, keyboardist and about 11 singers standing on a low, level stage. My soul operated at an all-time low. My emotions ran high and I felt displaced, embarrassed and abandoned on all levels. Exposed.

I was falling apart at my job. I couldn't concentrate. My supervisor had suggested I go to church. It was a good sign that a couple of little children wanted to give me a high five, grin at me or just get my attention. Their innocent eyes gazed my way with wonder. Sunlight shined through stainedglass windows. They were interested in this white stranger.

It was a bright and sunny September day. I felt self-conscious but safe sitting in the congregation. After about an hour of music I was wondering when the preacher would begin his sermon. Just then the music subsided. The gray-haired preacher stepped to the lectern and began his sermon with a reminder that they still needed to raise some money for an upcoming event. Then, he began his sermon.

"Ladies and gentleman of the congregation, we have a soldier among us today. A soldier we will not see very often. This soldier has been waylaid and betrayed by someone very close to him. This soldier is a good man with a sorrowful soul. We will not let the evil-doers overtake this soldier." (Amen!)

I wondered if my supervisor had mentioned anything to the preacher about my situation, or was he just zoned in on me, and read my story somehow. Preachers are like that sometimes. I felt tears begin to burn in my eyes as the band began to rise as the preacher spoke to the congregation.

"We will not let the evildoers overtake this good soldier!" The church erupted. I was very moved by the time the band reached its crescendo. The organ unlocked something in my cells or my soul. Power and Glory working magic. This powerful hum lasted maybe three minutes. Soon, I felt I needed to get some fresh air. I stood up and walked toward the door. There are times when only faith exists because outside facts or forces cannot be controlled or altered. A little old black lady with white hair said, "Don't leave yet. Read this passage with me." She ran her dark fingers unders the lines as the preacher read. When he was finished, she touched my arm and said, "God be with you, son."

The bright sun illuminated my walk back to the car after that Sunday service. Things looked up for a week or so just from that one day as if I possessed a golden mojo.

Electric Blue

Above the mirror behind a liquor display, a blue neon beer sign flickered and dimmed while Luke Tarver sat at the bar. He enjoyed watching Amanda, the lovely brunette bartender, distracted by the annoying flicker of the neon light. Beautiful confusion on her face proved worth the price of any beer. Amanda's cruel curvaceous body drove most men to distraction. Her face reminded him of some killer-eyed beauty from those high quality fashion magazines.

Luke knew she'd never correlate the bothersome sign with his presence. Since he discovered no wedding ring on Amanda's finger some time ago, he considered revealing his secret to her. Luke acted like he read the newspaper while she waited on her share of admiring customers in the early evening hour.

His grandmother possessed a similar inexplicable force. No watch operated on his grandmother's wrist. It never mattered how new, expensive or inexpensive the watchit never kept time while on her wrist, and it remained a family mystery.

"Hey, how are you?"

"I'm fine. Looks like you're busy this evening."

"A little bit. What can I get you?"

"I'll have a Guinness."

Luke struggled not to stare at Amanda. He watched her glance toward the flickering neon. He smoked a cigarette while perusing the sports page. She brought the stout and gave him a smile as he handed her a twenty dollar bill. Luke felt lost in this woman. He looked back at the paper.

He remembered the first time he recognized the extent of his mysterious gift. When he was a kid he could pick fourleaf clovers out of the lawn by pointing to them. This phenomenon he could articulate to no one. Later, he noticed a strange coincidence that street lamps often dimmed in his presence. Only when he was old enough to walk the streets alone could he verify this strange fact.

Luke rarely drew this phenomenon to people's attention. He didn't completely understand his power of channeling energy, insight, or foreknowledge and he always thought something might be wrong with him to invoke this mystical telepathyat times he thought he could even hear what people were thinking.

This strange psychic element remained a heavy burden because people he confided in often refused to believe the truth when he told it to them. His insight was a double-edged sword, but the feeling he carried with him remained opposite of an inborn fear.

Luke discovered in certain instances, radio frequencies became disrupted by his presence. The frequencies became disturbed when he felt in a positive mood, being carefree and unself, conscious. His mysterious gift appeared when it was least expected and often unwanted.

"Another stout?" asked Amanda after thirty minutes, pouring what remained from the bottle into his glass.

"Yes, one more," he replied glancing up at the flickering sign to remind her it still wasn't functioning properly. A regular barfly called out to Amanda and she walked to the other end of the bar to fetch the customer a draft beer just as Luke wanted to begin a conversation with her.

Luke waited on Freddie, who was late, as usual. Freddie, an old friend of Luke's who sometimes used Luke for his insight, planned an evening out on the town tonight.

Years earlier, Freddie invited several friends over to his house. In those days Freddie was an avid music enthusiast. For two months Freddie knew the Silvertones were being broadcast live on the radio and it was Freddie's intention to record the performance. A strong local frequency comforted Freddie. He planned everything he kept three different stereo systems in his house to record the show, but the main stereo in the living room had the strongest signal.

That night, while Luke stood in the middle of the hardwood living room floor, in front of the entertainment center, they noticed reception dulled and faded while Luke stood in the room.

"That shouldn't be happening with this antenna," uttered a concerned Freddie a few minutes before showtime.

Without resistance or negativity, Luke noticed his slightest movement altered the radio's signal. He began to jest, intentionally disturbing the frequency, by moving his arm in the slightest direction, laughing. "How in the hell are you doing that?" asked Freddie. Even though Freddie stood amazed at this phenomenon, he wouldn't allow Luke in the living room during the performance that night.

The bar filled up. Luke could no longer pretend to read the paper. He watched Amanda. She wore shorts in the mild December weather, showing her beautiful long legs. The tight tee shirt revealed a striking anatomy. Instead of her usual ponytail, today her long, wavy dark hair hung down below her shoulders. Amanda's smile attracted many drinkers. Her eyes were as blue as two pristine swimming pools. Luke began to notice Amanda watching him out of the corner of her eye.

"I've never had stout," Amanda said to Luke when she made her way back to him. Her wide blue eyes were mesmerizing.

"It's health food, y'know."

"Health food?"

"I'm only kidding, but it's good to drink before a meal."

"I'll have to drink one and try it out," she said, smiling a telling glance as if she knew a secret, and he didn't. She made Luke wish she knew his secret. Local barflies continued vying for Amanda's attention for drink or otherwise. Luke didn't mind Freddie was running late since Amanda tended bar this evening. When she was called away by a young-looking patron, Luke walked to the bathroom. When he returned the neon light resumed flickering.

"What's the deal with that light?" he asked Amanda, drawing her attention toward the neon sign. "It's never done this before. It's definitely getting on my nerves."

She stared at the electric sign for a moment. He admired her long, dark eyelashes and her sly grin struck him to the bone. Luke felt effects of the stout on his empty stomach.

"If I told you I was making that light flicker, would you have dinner with me?"

"You're crazy."

"I've been called that before. Do you think I can make it go out?"

She pursed her lips, knitted her eyebrows and gave him a look as if maybe she believed him.

"No," she said playfully.

"If I make the light go out, will you?"

"Okay yes," she said with a smile. "And if you don't?"

"Bring me a Bass Ale, and by the time you pour the beer the light will be out," Luke uttered, attempting to make this beautiful woman who looked to be nearing his age, of around thirty, realize this was all meant to happen. He stepped back from the bar where the electric currency seemed strongest. She brought the beer, and just then Freddie made his grand entrance.

"Amanda, that is a dangerous character you're consorting with. You should be very careful around this man."

When Freddie sat down, Amanda said, "He's promised to turn off the neon beer sign without touching it."

"My dear girl, I hope you didn't bet with something you couldn't pay."

When she looked up, the light was out. Luke and Amanda exchanged glances. She laughed and said, "I get off work in an hour."

She returned to waiting on customers as if their deal never happened.

"You sonofabitch," said Freddie, sitting down next to Luke at the bar.

"Hey, she's my favorite bartender," Luke said.

"You know you can't go out with her tonight."

"What?"

"We've got business."

"You heard the lady. I only have one hour. All I have to do is sit back, not puke on myself, and listen to the jukebox until then."

"We'll be back in time."

"Fred, look at her."

"Come on, this is why we met here, it's close to the track."

"Don't give me that shit. Motherfucker, if you'd show up on time for once, we'd already be gone. You gave me a chance to work my courage up. Tomorrow I'll pick a winner; I'm not focusing on horses now, and besides you never reap luck on Thursdays anyway."

"You're gonna squander your talent on a woman?" Luke only looked at his friend without responding.

"Okay, scratch that, but you can always get a date with her. I'm starting to believe your only weakness is women."

"So, it's settled. We're going to the track tomorrow."

"Well, listen ol' boy. I already told Malcolm I'd put five hundred on the Bound To Fade."

"You what?"

"You told me yesterday you had a feeling."

"You're pushing too hard. I never said to make that bet."

"Fuck, Luke, that's my rent money. I'll be evicted if I'm late again. Don't let me down."

"Let you down? Hey, you jumped the gun, I told you..."

"Great, I'm fucked. Thanks for nothing." Freddie stormed out of the bar.

...

When Amanda's shift ended, she asked him when they walked outside to his truck, "Are you going to tell me how you turned that light off?"

"Asking the magician to reveal his tricks, eh?"

They went to dinner, and an instant connection transcended time between them.

"Does your friend Fred have a gambling problem?"

"Well...let's just say he likes taking chances."

"How did you let him down? Not that it's my business." Her voice trailed off, and then she said, "But you getting that light to turn out is my business," and gave him a smile that would turn any good man's blood to wine. Her white teeth were perfect. The lips irresistible...

Although he stayed private about it normally, Luke felt a sense of ease and relief about sharing his story, and Amanda without further questioning, smiled and said, "I believe you, Luke Tarver. Do you not like to talk about it?"

"Not unless I want people to think I'm nuts," he said lightheartedly.

"Fair enough."

A few hours later Luke and Amanda rode along in Luke's new truck and they noticed a drunken and unkempt Freddie stumbling down Elizabeth Street. Luke parked by a curb near his friend.

"Well, well, well. If it ain't the date that couldn't wait."

"Fred, where you been?"

"Well, I'm trying to decide where I'm gonna pawn my stereo equipment and music collection, but I think I need a few more drinks to figure it out."

"Let's go get a six-pack," said Luke, allowing Freddie to climb in the small back seat of the truck. They drove off and Luke noticed Amanda roll her window down a bit to diminish Freddie's unwashed scent.

"So, you guys already have a couple-ish glow.

Amanda, has Luke told you about his freakish power yet?"

"I've seen a couple examples." She smiled and then looked at Luke who gave her an approving nod.

"Oh yeah, the electric blue neon sign," Freddie muttered.

Luke left them talking in the car while he ran into the liquor store. He bought a sixpack of tall Budweisers, a big bag of cashews, and three scratchoff lottery tickets. Luke climbed back into his truck and handed the tickets to Freddie and said, "Here, scratch these off. I believe you're a winner."

Freddie began scratching the tickets. He loved the thrill of gambling.

"Nothing on that one," he said, throwing the old ticket on the floorboard, moving to the next one licking his lips. Amanda and Luke glanced at each other and smiled as Freddie scratched the next ticket, and after a few seconds he began yelling, "Holy fucking aces, Luke, you just won a thousand dollars. Check those numbers and make sure I'm reading it right."

"This ticket is a confirmed winner," uttered Amanda, now looking at Luke with a gaze of wild wonder. Freddie rubbed his hands together in fiendish delight.

After a few moments of silence, Luke said, "Fred, take the money and get your rent together."

"What? Oh shit, you're kidding me! You mean it?

You've saved my ass again, Luke, thanks so much brother. Unless you're fucking with me..."

"Take the money, but don't ever give me that guilt trip shit again. I think we should suspend our gambling for a while after today."

"You're quitting?"

"I'm tired of all the stress it brings."

Freddie realized staring at Luke and Amanda together in the front seat that times were changing. Their gaze said it all...

"I'll never question you again. But for the Kentucky Derby next spring maybe we could have some fun. But damn, talking about stress...shit, Luke, you're gonna hate finding real work."

The Bayou Sideshow

"I shouldna' been foolin' with a married man," uttered our hero, Doreen, as she grinned a perfect smile and passed me the pipe.

"I'll have to go back to the beginning for you to understand the disturbing circumstances I got myself into...he never told me he was married."

We sat around an antiquated oak table in Doreen's small den. She called her small abode the "den of iniquity." Incense and candles burned throughout the small, low-ceilinged room. The candles flickered strange shapes upon the walls. A scent of pine and cinnamon wafted throughout the house. Arabic rugs covered the floors. The smell of December woodsmoke lingered throughout this comfortable house while howling winter winds gently shook its doors and windows.

Doreen, a gracious soul whose countenance emanated good cheer that served as medicine to the bones, was in her late thirties. Divorced. Childless. Her charm and wit appealed to everyone. Doreen was a hair designer who dyed her long hair coal black. Her brown eyes were inviting. She wore one silver ring on her right hand.

Her smile provided serenity on the eve of resuming my travels west. She confessed this story in the spirit of warding off negative forces during my journey.

"I was still working at the bar during this time. These traveling carpenters would come through town y'know, and I hooked up with this guy. We had us a big ol' time. He worked in town for a few weeks. When his job was over, he went home.

"He invited me to visit him in Louisiana. So, a couple of weeks later, I bought a plane ticket and flew into Baton Rouge from Atlanta.

"As soon as I step off the plane, things begin to get strange. The guy I was foolin' with, his name was Will, wasn't at the airport to pick me up. But his friend Roy was, and he picked me right out of the crowd. Roy had a girlfriend with him. Talk about a couple. Good ol' Roy informs me, he said, 'Will is hung up with his wife. He'll be over later.'

"I'm thinking wife? He's married? I knew then I was in trouble.

"So, we drive in Roy's old 76' sky blue Ford pickup truck, almost sixty miles into the bayou. I mean, the middle of nowhere. A dense, swampy jungle. Everything looked the same. No signs. No nothing. Just swamp.

"Once we got into the bayou, everything took on this strange undercurrent, like some kind of voodoo. It was creepy. It always felt like something was watching me.

"Roy is drinking tall Budweisers the entire time. He was a short, ugly fellow. His brown hair was long in the back, crew cut on top, and he had a nasty looking moustache. He had farmer-tanned arms tattooed with various home-made India ink designs. His truck reeked like sweat, nicotine and stale beer mixed with a whiff of cheap cologne trying to mask it all over.

"I could not bring myself to say anything. I could only wait. Worry was no good. I felt helpless. I was so pissed at myself for, once again, getting into such a desperate situation...this guy, Will, led me to believe he had some money.

"We get to Roy's place. Talk about a white-trash scenario. The trailer was lined with thick, bright orange shag carpet. It smelled like unwashed feet in there. Sour mold.

"At this point I became annoyed. I called Will. No answer. I ask Roy if I can take a shower. He says sure. The June heat was festering. I asked if I could use a towel. 'Ain't there one innair?' His towel looked like a mechanic's rag. Luckily, I had my own towel, but I hated the idea of unpacking my clothes in this freak's trailer.

"I get out of the shower, and I'm sweating all over again. By the time I get dressed, I discover Roy is gone.

"I call Will for a couple of hours. No answer of course. I start to get worried. I start thinking I may never see this guy.

"A couple of hours later, Roy returns, tall Budweiser in hand, and says, 'Will cain't git away from the wife. She ain't leavin town like he figured. Not tonight anyways.'

"Roy wanted to go out. What else could I do? Of course, I should've left town because after that everything just got crazy.

"We get in Roy's truck and drive through dense swampland for miles. It's all still looking the same cypress trees and swamp water in every direction you look. Sure, it's beautiful in a way, but if you ever get lost, you're in trouble because there's no sense of direction. Even my sense of time was lost.

"After what seemed to be twenty miles of dirt road, we pull into this narrow, gravel driveway, passing a rusted sign that said The Ramble Inn. It was a decrepit shack, hidden from the road. I never could have found my way out of there. It became obvious I was not leaving Louisiana on my own. I was gonna need help.

"A few scattered trucks were parked out front. Broken bottles and old rusted cars were all around. Let me tell you, I've never seen a place like this. The damn place had dirt floors! Dirt floors! The walls were fake wood paneling. There were two pool tables, and some broken electric bowling game. The clientele looked like refugees from a government experiment.

"Roy knew everyone there, and I suppose I felt safe as a stranger could in that place. It was the most seedy, rundown shack I've ever stepped inside. This situation was insane and all too real, but I knew I had to relax and ride this thing out. I drank a couple of beers out of a cooler to take the edge off.

"Everyone tried to be accommodating. Soon, a few of Roy's friends sit down to play their ritual game of Friday night poker. All these ol' boys just adored me because I had my real teeth. They thought I had to be a Hollywood movie star because I didn't have no 'store bought' teeth, as they called them.

"Meanwhile, these guys are rolling joints and smoking them in this dank shack. I'm talking strong smoking reefer, the kind that makes a room smell like a skunk just by opening the bag.

"Then this ol' boy comes in and sits down next to me at the table. The guy is another friend of Roy's. Short, skinny, kinda quiet fellow. I tell the guy after he asks, I'm not playin' cards, just here to watch.

"They kept calling him Halfbrain. Funny-looking guy.

He answers to this nickname without question, as if he heard it many times. I just thought they called him that because of some inside joke. I wasn't about to ask questions. These guys spoke among themselves with references to the card game.

"Halfbrain is not playing cards. He starts talking to me. He wondered how long I was going to be in town. This guy gave me a dumb smile and said he wanted to take me to the 'free supper.' I had no idea what the free supper entailed, and there was no way I'd make such a commitment, so I just kept a general flow of conversation going. Everything led back to the fact I had no business being there. I blundered in a big way. I told Halfbrain where I was from and all, why I was there.

"After several beers, a few joints and too many rounds of poker to count from Roy and the boys, I mustered enough courage to ask my new friend why they called him Halfbrain. He smiled and immediately removed his railroad cap. Half of his forehead was missing!

"He explained 'See, I was packing the gun too tight and the gun fired. It blew part of my head off.' I could not help but stare a minute. My jaw dropped, but everyone else kept playing cards like they heard the story a thousand times before.

"By this time, the fading late afternoon sunlight only cast a shadow through the front door of The Ramble Inn. That light coming through the front door was my only way to calibrate the time of day.

"Halfbrain put his hat back on. He was talking to me like he knew me for years, especially after revealing the most important event in his life. He seemed to have a shine for me. He made me nervous, but everything there made me nervous. I resigned myself to cling to anything that would get me out of this place because still no Will.

"Halfbrain told me, just like I'm telling you, a story about how he killed a man. Halfbrain said it really wasn't like killing a real person, since the guy was a 'neegra.' Halfbrain said the guy was fooling around with his wife, so he killed him. Halfbrain told me how he waited for the guy outside his apartment. How he shot him. How the dude fell into the bushes. He told the story just like I'm telling you this now. There was no way he could've been making it up.
He really confided in me. He said the cops never caught him.

"Y'know, to him it was just another common story of murder among these folks. It seemed some kind of backwoods ethic existed there. Ain't no law around, so they operate on a contraband code... Horrible... Horrifying... All along, these ol' boys are playing cards, passing around this religious reefer that would give you sticky fingers.

"It had to be close to midnight when Roy's girlfriend finally arrives to drive us back to the trailer. Roy was too drunk to drive. We hardly spoke. I rode in a delirium. I couldn't believe the craziness unfolding around me. Of course, I was the only one who felt this crowd was strange.

The Local Stranger

"That night, I had to sleep on the nasty shag carpet along with the mysterious stains and scents that were imbedded in the cheap fibers. Knowing that Roy and his girlfriend were sleeping together just on the other side of a thin plastic door just drove me crazy.

"As I slept, if you want to call it that, in a stone cold fever, I had this recurring dream, the trailer is rolling down the road out of control, and Halfbrain is running behind the trailer trying to save me.

"At ten o'clock the next morning on Saturday, Will finally shows up at the trailer. He explains to me how sorry he is about the whole situation, but that we may not be able to each other tonight, or any during the weekend.

"I cussed that son of a bitch out like I ain't ever cussed anyone out before, but he just drove off in a cloud of dust. I was fit to be tied. Oh, I was pissed. I wanted to leave that damn bayou then and there.

"In the trailer, the phone, of course, mysteriously doesn't work. It's dead. I'm beginning to panic. I couldn't stay in that dump. I decided to go look for a phone. I grab my overnight bag and walk out of the trailer. Getting a taxi and going home are my intentions. Roy was still asleep. I didn't want to bother with him, and the girlfriend's car was gone anyway. I was still so pissed.

"I walked from yesterday's memory, up to a dirt road in search of a pay phone. No cars in sight, and it's Saturday to boot. I must've walked for two or three miles.

"I began to cry because I didn't believe I was ever gonna get out of that place. It was so hot with no breeze at all. I felt like I'd been dipped in heated oil. It seemed like everything in the swamp was alive and watching me. It was a nightmare being stranded alone in the swamp, lost. I was expecting some animal to charge out of the woods and devour my ass right there. Finally, thank God, I stumbled upon a pay phone outside some crossroad convenience store. By then, I was drowning in despair.

"I called my sister, crying hysterically. I just wanted to go home so bad. I was freaking out. My sister kept asking me where I was, but I couldn't tell her. I had no idea. I was in the middle of the swamp. In the background, I heard my smartass brother say 'Tell her to call 911, they'll be able to find her!'

"I knew there were no taxis within twenty or thirty miles. The store was closed. There was no one to ask questions. I couldn't stand being there alone.

"I got mad at myself again. I had no choice but to walk back to Roy's and see if he would take me to the airport. I was so frustrated that I nearly felt insane. All along, I'm still carrying my suitcase.

"So, I trudged back to the trailer. It was past two o'clock when I got there. I opened the door, and there is Roy and Halfbrain drinking tall Budweisers. I was delirious. They insisted on getting more beer. Roy informed me I should stick around. 'Phones'll be fixed, and Will is supposed to call back in a bit.'

"The three of us climb into Roy's truck. Halfbrain lets me know, if my plans fall through, he would take me to the 'free supper' tonight. If my plans fall through?

"Roy informs me he is taking me to a very special watering hole. He fires up one of those strong smoking joints for the ride while the sun's heat and glare provided a mischievous and increasing intensity.

"I can't remember the name of the bar, but at least the place had wooden floors. It was then I realized I'd not eaten since I left Georgia. I was starved. We sat at the bar. They ordered beers. I asked for a menu. They were out of everything I wanted to eat so I had to settle for a grilled cheese sandwich. I felt that was a safe bet.

"While we were waiting, Halfbrain and Roy talked with the other locals. Everyone knew everyone else.

"Finally the grilled cheese arrived. Worst grilled cheese ever. Soggy white bread. Hard cheese. Even the chips were stale. I felt cursed at this point.

"Country music played on the jukebox. Chicken wire was built around a little stage for live entertainment. It looked like they had no bands in quite some time. All sorts of strange folks loitered about.

"At least today there were a few females to balance the bar's population. Roy talked to some bleached blonde. Halfbrain walked out to the truck with his case of beer. I kept an eye on Roy, because I didn't want to get stranded. He kept putting his hand on the bleached blonde's ass.

"Then this big guy walks into the place—big, greasy, redbearded, longhaired, mean-looking guy. The dude has this ugly ass pit bulldog on a leash with scars all over it. Vicious looking fucker. The guy sits at the corner of the bar just two seats down from me. The down-home waitress at the bar, pencil behind her ear, hand on her hip, says in a bored tone as if she were accustomed to such nonsense,'Frankie, you cain't bring that damn dog in here.'

'Aw Loretta, he don't want nuthin' to eat.' "The waitress reconsiders and says,'Well awright then,' and she returned to her waitress duties.

"Halfbrain comes back in, says hello to Frankie, and starts in on me about the 'free supper' tonight. We sat in that place for what seemed to be the longest time. By now, Roy is blind drunk. He can't drive. He says a friend will drive him home. Then, Halfbrain declares he'd drive Roy's truck to the 'free supper.' "Halfbrain would hear nothing of taking me to the airport. 'Stay awhile,' he kept saying. I felt a desperation I've never known since then.

"I drank a couple of beers. Roy disappeared with the bleached blonde. Halfbrain wouldn't allow me to refuse the 'free supper' invitation. I was stranded. A slave to circumstance. Halfbrain was my only hope of getting out of there, and that wasn't a comfortable realization.

"We finally get to this 'free supper,' which is being held in a tent. Folks are spooning out spaghetti and fried chicken. It was a strange combination, but I was starving.

"The chicken tasted like wood. I didn't bother eating the spaghetti. It was a disgusting, runny mess. No wonder it was free. I ate a couple of dry rolls out of starvation while Halfbrain said, 'Told ye this'd be good.'

"At this point, I felt so far from anything in my life I was familiar with. These people were, I don't know, so cut off, rural, unsteady, backward, and this is coming from a person who was raised in the country, mind you. It's hard to explain. I found myself staring out into the blackness of the bayou, but that only chilled me with the cold realization that I was in a definite unknown.

"So at the end of this free supper, these ol' boys start talking about dogfighting. They spoke as if it were a wellknown event that was about to occur. Tonight! No one there it seemed, except me, was an outsider. Things became stranger by the minute.

"Of course, I reminded myself it was nobody's fault but mine that I landed in this position. Had I known Will was married, I'd never bought the ticket. All this was selfinflicted misery.

"It was dark by the time we drove to a part of the bayou where the locals hide with the intention of never being found. My fear returned with a gravity and force I could no longer ignore. Beer didn't help. Nothing calmed my nerves.

"I knew dogfighting was illegal, so I knew the people there had to be at least as crazy as Halfbrain. I was, naturally, very worried. We drove for miles farther into the dense swamp. I mean, I'm in the swamp with a guy, maybe a confessed killer they call Halfbrain, going to a dogfight.

"I had a bad feeling. The dirt roads were only a few feet from rising swamp water; the slightest swerve and you're gone.

"We arrived at an open field near some water. There was a strange excitement in the air. All these trucks with dog cages in the back, parked around this huge pit.

"The pit was a few feet below ground level. The wooden borders in the pit were stained with blood from previous fights. Those poor dogs. I felt horrified. I missed my dog. I nearly began to cry right there.

"It was one of those perverse moments of terror as I watched the animals try to kill each other. You could feel the wicked undercurrents of violence and mindless cruelty in these people. Money and whiskey transformed them. And the blood, too. It was sickening, but I said nothing. Since I was an outsider, I thought they might just kill me and dump me in the swamp.

"There was no regard for those dogs that lost. Owners killed their dogs on the spot. They threw the dead bodies in a Dumpster. It was terrible. I told Halfbrain I wanted to leave, that I was feeling sick. Halfbrain drove me back to the trailer. I must say, he did watch out for me.

"I could not sleep that night. That Dumpster was full of dead dogs. I still couldn't get that picture out of my mind. I lay balled up on the floor, looking at my watch every twenty minutes. My bones were chilled and my chest was tight like a cold was coming on. I wanted to scream, but I knew I had to hold myself together.

"I saw every aspect of my life in a different light. All the seasons and nostalgia of my life passed before my eyes. I promised if I ever got out of this bayou sideshow, I'd never fool with another married man again.

"At six o'clock on Sunday morning, I woke Roy up. Seeing the sun come up in such a place made me sick with myself. I told Roy I would pay him one hundred dollars if he would drive me to the airport. Right then. Right now. 'Okay. But how much beer do we have?' is the first thing he asks.

"So, Roy and his girlfriend, not the bleached blonde, but the first one, emerge from the bed space to drive me to the airport. This girlfriend, Denise, smacked her bubble gum the entire drive.

"I couldn't believe I was finally on my way to the airport. The fact I had to wait several hours for a flight did not bother me in the least. Denise just smacked her gum and talked about nothing the entire time. She acted as if she had no idea Roy left with the bleached blonde last night. Or maybe she did.

"They were real nice to me on the way to the airport, saying things like, 'Sorry there was a misunderstanding, next time you come, we'll getcha a motel.' I nearly shouted, 'What next time? I ain't ever coming back to this crazy fucking place! They really believed I had a good time. They took the one hundred dollars, too!

"When I got back home the shit didn't end. All my friends and family especially my brother kidded me for weeks, asking when I was heading back to 'Loozeanner'?

"Get this...and then not a month later, I get a letter from the Louisiana Women's Correctional Facility. Turns out, Roy's girlfriend, Denise, wrote me from there. I think I still have the letter somewhere.

"Denise wrote about how Roy abused her. How they became strung out on crack. How she was in a mental facility because she couldn't afford drug treatment. In the letter, she said I was her best friend in the whole world, and that she loved me like a sister. Funny thing is, we hardly spoke fifty words to each other the entire time I was there.

"Anyway, that's the last time I've heard, and hope to hear, from those crazy folks. That trip was my heart of darkness. It was the strangest time of my life, chasing a married carpenter into the depths of the bayou. I learned the hard way, the swamp ain't no place for outsiders."

Brother To Jackals

I have become a brother to jackals,
a companion of owls.
Job 30:29

Like a muddied spring or a polluted well,
is a righteous man who gives way to the wicked.
Proverbs 25:26

A coward friend makes a valiant foe.
Herman Melville

To live outside the law, you must be honest.
Bob Dylan

He tasted blood on his lips. He never saw the punch coming, and when it landed square on his mouth a metallic taste of anger singed his mind. In a cold rage blind instincts gripped his senses as he gritted his teeth and smashed Richard Fleshman in the windpipe. Fleshman bent over with his hands clenching his throat. Bar stools scattered across the floor. A beer bottle crashed at his feet.

For a long time some obscure intuition reminded him an event like this would eventually transpire scuffling on the barroom floor of The Neon Eel. Floodgates of released frustration opened into perverse action. Flickering lights composed his blurred vision. Broken glass lie scattered across the floor like worthless deadly diamonds. As they struggled, he could hear Crazy Annie screaming: "Stomp the motherfucker's brains out, Fleshman!"

After attempting to snatch Fleshman's ponytail from his head, he began prying Fleshman's eyeball from the right socket when they were pulled apart. He felt blood on his chin. He may have broken a tooth.

He understood, feeling a sharp pain in his hand, this situation occurred because he kept time with ruinous companions. Times like these made him forget what he liked about this place. He finally discovered the severe price of betraying his instincts.

It didn't matter to anyone that Fleshman threw the first punch. A sucker punch to the mouth. Fleshman proved knocked out loaded, in a notorious drunken tirade, employing his proclivity to insult people. From the beginning of their acquaintance Fleshman often sported him as a scapegoat.

The fighters were pulled apart in a crowd of leering patrons hungry for the spill of barroom blood and guided to separate ends of the bar. Each man sat consoled by various sidetakers. Shouted insults could not be heard over commotion and animated drunkenness that escalated and finally subsided after a short while.

He felt stares from strangers, streaking an evil gall in his veins. His whirling, disorienting anger rendered him unable to read the Budweiser clock behind the bar. Sam Tanner laid a thick, hairy arm around his lean shoulders. It made him feel better to know Sam stood by his side since he felt certain downtown acquaintances siding against him. This evening lingered like a bad dream, cheap drama. He could hear the gossip now. He felt verifications of old truths resurfacing. He ignored blood dripping from his hand onto the floor. He must've fallen on a broken bottle.

"Why do you let him get to you?" asked the corpulent Sam Tanner, who lived with Fleshman at the Junk House.

"He fucking sucker punched me." He spat blood on the dusty floor, tonguing his cut lip, but he lost no teeth.

"You were wailing on him pretty good. Let me get us a drink. Hey, Doreen! Let me and m'boy get four shots of Cuervo. And a towel! You're bleeding, brother."

"I'm sick of that motherfucker's shit."

"You still have some blood on your chin too."

They did not speak again until Doreen poured tequila into four shot glasses on the old wooden bar.

"Sam, it looks like he needs stitches," Doreen said, handing him a towel.

A few lighthearted jokes passed as bar activity gradually returned to normal. The alienation he felt made his blood wise.

"Doreen, darlin, one more double round. Hey man, we should take you to the emergency room for that hand."

"I ain't goin' to no fuckin' emergency room."

Sam pulled on his moustache and watched his friend stare at his own blood dripping on the floor.

"You're a tough fucker. You know that Fleshman wishes he could do what you do, but he can't...still, you gotta see about that hand, brother. The lip, too."

"I ain't goin' to no emergency room."

The deep gash in his hand spread open, and bled. Smeared blood stained his faded blue jeans. As Sam said, he felt a strange shame for lowering to such a foolish level, but he refused to allow the sucker punch to go unanswered. He was already feeling a dread of living with haunting consequences from this poisonous folly.

"Fuck you all!" Fleshman yelled, reeling out of the bar in a grand exit, but perverse tension still hung in the air. Cantina eyes looked his way. He heard Crazy Annie speaking in a conspiring tone a stage whisper to one of her bar hag cronies.

He swallowed the last tumbler of tequila, and stumbled out of the bar into the cold winter air toward home with a bloody white towel wrapped around his left hand.

1

A full moon hung in the sky like some mad voyeur on a second Wednesday of the month. A tall, large-boned man with black kinky hair walked into The Stray Cat Lounge on this cold, clear December night. A Mexican disco album blared over the club speakers. Clouded cigarette smoke floated above the rafters. The man walked into the bar and glanced toward a booth where the familiar individual sat waiting for this clandestine ritual to begin.

They greeted each other with slight nods. An uneasy chemistry flowed between the men. The large man sat down and stared into the eyes of a cold-blooded public servant. Tonight, the informant felt resigned to his fate as he waited for the familiar questioning, sitting like a seduced rodent mesmerized by the quiet, precise stalking of a serpent.

The public servant, Rosco Williams, pulled a pack of Marlboro reds from his faded bluejean jacket. He wore green fatigue army pants. Williams chose a random cigarette from the pack and lit it with a gold military lighter. The two men avoided eye contact while ordering beers from a longlegged brunette waitress.

"You're running outta time friend," spoke Williams, exhaling smoke, watching the impotent individual sitting across from him.

"These things take time," muttered the informant, peeling at the blue label of his beer bottle.

"I didn't put you in this situation. You got busted. Either way, you're fucked. It's information or jail. You know the game."

As the waitress brought their beers, the informant realized with a nauseous clarity that his entire life burned toward this heinous ruin. He noticed the scar over Williams's left eye. For so long this informant ran when not pursued; paranoia and fatigue festered upon his spirit, reaping demons with rampant claims for his soul with no place to hide. He traveled on a long road to nowhere haunted by a fevered madness saturating his soul with a sick confidence.

Life narrowed to a moment when the past, present and future constellations aligned. His lack of faith had propelled him into the position of a Judas goat. He watched car lights stream down the familiar nighttime streets decorated for the season. The disco beat and flickering bar lights annoyed him, and the holidays brought him no cheer.

"So, who is turning the zombie dust?" asked Williams with beer suds matted on his black moustache, flicking his cigarette ashes on the floor, intent on obtaining all the information he needed by the time he finished his beer.

"Marty Saulings and Lester Hilgram are the only two I can think of."

"Bullshit."

"Man, far as I can tell the Junk House boys don't deal."

"Bullshit! Listen, they're turning something. You know it and I know it. They get the shit from someone with serious connections."

"I can only do so much. They're supposed to be friends of mine."

"Listen you fucking idiot. You don't have any friends except me. Understand?" Williams's face turned an irascible red. He spoke through gnashed teeth.

"This ain't right. You can't do this," uttered the informant.

"I can do whatever I want. I don't give a shit. I'll fuck you where you breathe. You got busted, so you play by my rules."

"Man, I could expose your ass."

Williams grabbed the informant by the collar before he could blink, turning his fist until the informant's jugular bulged. "You don't seem to fucking understand. I have the authority to put you away for drug dealing because I am an officer of the law. My friends are lawyers and judges who are your worst fucking enemies. Now, if you want to fuck up, that's okay, because you've lost your friends since you made your deal with me. Consequently, you narrowed your choice to this: if you don't get the story on the Junk House gang, I'll make sure you're flayed like a dog in the street. You'll never see the light of day again. I'll always have more evidence than you."

"Listen. I'll get something. I hate Fleshman, but you can't rush this shit. They never have dealer's money. They're just addicts."

Williams released the informant's collar. He drank almost all of his Natural Lite in one swallow. He smashed his cigarette butt in a black plastic ashtray.

"That's not good enough." Williams quaffed the rest of his beer. He pulled a yellow envelope from his jean jacket and slid it across the table to the informant.

"Take this money and make a buy with them, a couple of eight balls. Do what you want with the rest."

"Blood money."

"Call it what you want. If I were you, I'd call it rent."

The informant tore open the yellow envelope under the table. He counted ten one-hundred dollar bills. "You need to have something on tape two weeks from today."

Williams said nothing else as he dropped a dollar for gratuity on the table, and walked out of the Stray Cat Lounge without looking back.

The money rested in the informant's pocket. He wished he could just leave town. He felt a despondent strangeness, as if his soul searched with nowhere to hide from the enormity of his transgressions. Even the brunette waitress avoided him.

His circumstance left him feeling exposed and recognized as an imposter. A phony. A liar. Contaminated. Tainted. He realized, everything, at one time or another, transforms into its opposite with nowhere to turn. He sold out his friends, and the cops didn't care if he went to jail. Finishing the beer, he left a tip and walked out into the cold evening to find Sam Tanner.

2

Jesse Wages awoke to a bone-colored December sun. Light crept through the window burning his eyes as he rolled off the old mattress and looked at himself in a mirror hanging on the wall. Bloodshot blue eyes revealed the story of another passing day.

He heard children playing in hallways of the dilapidated apartment building. He wiped sweat from his face and forehead with a towel. When he returned to his bedroom, Jesse pulled open a drawer of his makeshift desk, and gathered ritual instruments of his vice: a plastic bag containing a sweet, tarlike puddy; another bag of potent marijuana and a water pipe. Today marked his day off from work. He basked in the security of awakening to a fresh and copious stash of rare, potent opium.

Jesse smoked in a languid grace easing his unsettled stomach. After feverish sleep, he strained to recollect what transpired last night. Then he remembered all those shots with Sully at the bar. Birds chirped outside the window. He felt disconnected with everything around him, but the dull sunlight relaxed him. He exhumed from his jean pants pockets containing three crumpled dollar bills, a pocket notebook, a matchbook, and forty-two cents.

He burned up his time in a wayward fashion these days. His work ethic disintegrated. Jesse hadn't written anything on his novel in weeks. He'd done very little lately, and now he began to feel like he was neglecting his skills.

He wondered, as he exhaled a thick cloud of blue illegal smoke, if today would conjure a newer revelation than yesterday. Days ran together in obscure discontent.

He reloaded the pipe and smoked again. A lonely awareness dawned on him as if transition floated in the air. He heard the black couple from across the hall arguing in the parking lot.

Jesse brushed his teeth. His roommate Sully already departed for work. The digital clock read 4:37 p.m.

Jesse dressed. He wore the same thermal underwear, blue Levi's and the gray flannel shirt as yesterday. He pulled on tan leather desert boots, put on an old corduroy jacket and walked across the street to see what was going on at the Junk House.

Outside, the cold air brought a clarity to his senses, an invigorated awareness. He heard a train moan in the distance. He noticed barelimbed trees standing as if stricken in horror under a frozen cobalt sky.

Jesse forgot to call Sara. She had left for work by now. He'd call her tonight.

He knocked on the battered Junk House door. The force of knocking pushed the unlocked door open. Jesse stuck his head inside and looked around only to notice Felix Mendoza resting on the couch in the living room. Felix had always displayed a nervous countenance, it seemed to Jesse, as if he were perpetually caught doing something wrong. He appeared to be watching a silent television. Felix was a big guy with black kinky hair. He always wore his sunglasses on an elastic cord around his neck.

Jesse asked, "Where's Sam?"

"He and Fleshman went downtown. You goin' to drink? Let me get my coat and I'll go with you." Felix slept on the couch these days at the Junk House. Jesse never asked Sam how well he knew Felix. Felix gave him the creeps. Jesse already regretted stopping by the house.

"I'm sort of in a hurry."

"To find Sam? I bet you are."

Jesse felt uncomfortable with Felix, who only acted friendly to him once no one else was around. On most occasions Felix never spoke to Jesse. They began walking toward the heart of town six or seven blocks away. Steam hushed from their mouths as they breathed in the cold wind.

"I heard you scored some of that mean opium. Very rare shit," mentioned Felix striding down Swiftsong Avenue toward The Neon Eel trying to keep up with Jesse's vigorous stride. The five o'clock sun faded fast on almost the shortest day of the year. Wisps of lavender and pink clouds resembled smoke floating toward the west.

"Who told you that?"

"Annie."

"She talks too fucking much."

"She didn't tell anyone else."

"Yeah. Of course not." Jesse tried to walk faster. He was never fond of revealing drug sources. The sound of Jesse's own boots on the sidewalk irritated him, much less Felix's intrusive conversation. Some esoteric instinct inside Jesse remained wary of Felix.

"I have a proposition for you," said Felix, completing Jesse's thoughts as they walked down a sloping sidewalk, passing familiar streets leading like capillaries to arteries of the town. A dead crepe myrtle stood like a skeleton in front of the Southern Belle flower shop they walked past.

"I'm sure this'll be enlightening."

"I'll walk in The Eel with you and see if Sam is around and I'll tell you there." Jesse felt Felix smothering his chance to shake his company. Felix reeked of some freaky desperation even more than usual.

They walked into The Neon Eel and sat on stools at the wooden bar. Today counted as Doreen's day off. Felix chainsmoked. No sign of Sam. Regulars and irritable drunks wandered around the bar in some midafternoon swagger. The familiar scent of sour alcohol, urine and disinfectant greeted patrons upon entering the bar.

Jesse ordered a stout. Felix ordered a vodka cranberry. Jesse decided to have one drink, wait on Sam, and then leave, shedding Felix.

"Well, y'know, I know the guy who supplies everyone with that once-in-a-lifetime opium you're smoking."

"I suppose it's always good to know people."

"My idea is you and I should pay the guy a visit." Jesse had already heard enough, but he felt curious as to what Felix might reveal to him. It seemed like inconsequential bar talk. He looked at Felix's pockmarked face. Felix's right leg never stopped jittering up and down.

"Why would We pay the guy a visit?" Jesse asked, catching a faint whiff of Felix-tinges of alcohol, nicotine, rotten teeth a sour scent of sweat, desperation and death that somehow overpowered the stench of The Eel.

"You and I are the only ones who know about this."

"Know about what?"

"Listen. The guy has a half an ounce of highgrade opium, and at least twenty thousand dollars in cash at his house."

"So?" Jesse sat, unable to follow the path Felix wanted to lead him down. Felix leaned closer to Jesse, as if someone in the empty bar might overhear. Felix's elbows rested on the bar.

"So, nobody knows that except you and me. The guy lives alone. We drive out there, come back and no one would ever know."

"Know what?"

"That we took the tar and cash from him."

"How do you intend taking his stash from him?" asked Jesse, only to hear an answer. Felix paused, looking at Jesse, a strange twitching occurring in the corner of his mouth.

"We kick the shit out of him. Or kill him," Felix muttered through an evil grin, dragging on his cigarette, staring at Jesse with viper eyes. His thick, black kinky hair remained matted and uncombed.

"You're fucking crazy."

"Listen man, I just went out there yesterday; the guy has twenty thousand dollars in a desk drawer. The stash is in a wooden cigar box in his closet. He lives so far out, no one would ever know."

"What do you mean no one would ever know? What are you talking about? If you killed him? Are you fucking stupid?" Jesse tried to finish his stout as quickly as possible.

Speaking in a lower tone, Felix half-whispered, "Strangle the motherfucker take his shit and haul ass. You wouldn't have to worry about where you're gonna get that shit for a while, because it's gonna be a long time before you see it again, and you'll have extra cash around for anything else." It made Jesse sick Felix confided such diseased ideas upon him.

"Count me out," Jesse said with a smile. "Anyway, you know you can't kill somebody and think that is going to be the end of it; as far as coppin' his stash, he's probably waiting for somebody like you to try some stupid shit like that anyway." Jesse was becoming angry with himself for continuing such a conversation.

"Well, maybe we could distract him and just steal the shit." Jesse was beginning to absorb Felix's seriousness for the first time. Felix ordered another drink. He lit a cigarette.

"No deal. Call John Gotti."

"Look, how much of that shit you got left?"

"Enough."

"Yeah. I bet. Enough."

"Well, it's a fucking idiotic idea. Why are you coming to me with this crazy shit?"

"Why not? The shit is illegal anyway. What's the difference? You're breaking the law by using the shit."

"You're talking about two very different things."

"You don't really believe that, do you?"

"Listen, Felix. Killing somebody is out of fucking control anyway you cut it. Even stealing it."

Felix smiled and took a sip of his drink. He then put his hand on Jesse's shoulder and said, "You're right. I don't want to hurt anyone, but its seems like some kind of golden opportunity...hell, Jesse, that's why I want you in on this. You're wise as a serpent." Jesse swilled his stout.

"Thanks, but no thanks."

Jesse dropped a dollar in the tip jar, and over his shoulder said: "You need to lay off that dust, and go get some sleep."

"C'mon, hang out awhile."

"I gotta go. Adios."

Jesse walked out of the bar. He headed home with the intention of remaining invisible to the locals. He knew the downtown temptation distracted him from his work, and he realized no shortage of temptations existed around here.

He felt good strolling down Crescent Avenue in the fresh air free from Felix. He smelled sandalwood. Change lingered in the air. He wondered what his roommate was up to at this hour.

3

Sully stood cooking an omelet in the kitchen when Jesse walked in the front door of their apartment. A smell of cheap cheese and butter wafted throughout the quarters, temporarily disguising other pungent scents emanating from their ramshackle building complex.

Sully's lit cigarette smoked in an ashtray on the kitchen table.

Old circus pictures hung on the walls. Bullet holes in the ceiling told tales of good times past. A sports talk show played on the radio. The cupboards above Sully's head tilted to one side, bordering on collapse.

Sully regarded his cooking habits with serious pride. He poured hot sauce in the skillet as Jesse closed the front door. Sully's thin, dark brown hair hung down to his shoulders. He wore torn and frayed blue jeans exposing stained thermal underwear, and the same Atlanta Braves tee shirt he had worn for the last three consecutive days. His old, sour-smelling Chuck Taylor tennis shoes had long since served their purpose. He turned and grinned a spooky tooth smile at Jesse. He sucked his fingers as he prepared his meal. That habit always made Jesse cringe a bit.

"Hell fire, boy, cooking up a storm in the kitchen, eh?" said Jesse, removing his windbreaker, and throwing it on the couch. The clock on the wall had not moved from 6:42 p.m. in several weeks. Sully's guitar sat propped up against the couch as if he'd just finished playing.

"I had a strange conversation with Felix today."

"I'd imagine. He's a strange guy. I never say much to him. You want some slop?"

"No thanks. Smells good, though. What's going on tonight?"

"I got a G from Sam."

"A whole one? I looked for him earlier when Felix fucking latched on to me. You want to split it?"

"Sure. Hey, who was that guy you were playing last night?"

"Dr. John."

"Oh, yeah. Dr. John."

Sully prepared his plate. He sucked at his fingers. Just as Sully walked back to his bedroom to eat, the phone rang. Sully picked it up. Jesse could tell by the way he spoke it must be Crazy Annie, Sully's latest girlfriend.

Jesse felt she only followed Sully around to become part of the local rock-and-roll tapestry Sully moved in. Crazy Annie bought him drugs to keep his company. She invested little in personal appearance. Her yellowish-stained teeth caught Jesse's eye every time she smiled between puffs of her cigarette. Her teeth and her loud barking laughs served as a reminder to Jesse of her true character lying beneath the surface.

Yet, she possessed a superficial charm at times that allowed her to navigate the rock-and-roll crowd like a pro.

Jesse smoked his pipe at the kitchen table, recalling how he and David "Sully" Sullivan cemented their friendship through a dedication to their craft. They shared an immense admiration for the same artists as well as sharing certain artistic vices.

This rare friendship served as an oasis for Jesse amid hipsters and fallen swingers that he perceived as seeking shortcuts to art by riding on the coattails of others through delusions of fortune, fame or drugs. For Jesse, their friendship existed on a higher level than downtown cliques, remaining impenetrable to outsiders. They met through a mutual friend years before. As the son of two teachers, Jesse graduated from the university while Sully barely got out of high school, they loved the same books and music. Their different upbringings aside, Jesse always felt that he and Sully shared much deeper connections that provided the source of inspiration for their daily endeavors.

Sully, a guitar-playing songwriter with a strong local following, was three years older than Jesse. The Silvertones, another local rock-and roll band that later gained national acclaim, covered several of Sully's songs on their early albums. It seemed to Jesse that Sully's songwriting credibility remained verified with the locals through this acknowledgement: If the "Tones" liked him well enough to do his songs then they might also follow his work.

Sully's small royalties couldn't pay all the bills, and they had often discussed how the rock and roll reality is rarely as it appears. Jesse deeply believed in Sully's talent. When Sully needed supplemental income, Jesse obtained him a job at the advertising agency where he worked.

Jesse exhaled the blue smoke and reflected on his friendship with Sully. They became friends from the first day they met as if they were childhood companions. After a mutual girlfriend introduced them one night years ago, they shared the seriousness of the other's artistic intention.

Early on, Jesse worried that Sully's lack of musical scope and variety, despite his acute ear, remained a flaw. So Jesse felt it served as his duty to protect his friend's weaknesses. Since he believed he and Sully had a mutual duty to assist in the others' artistic journey, he was open and honest concerning sharing poetic secrets.

Jesse wasn't calculating. He never used his insight against Sully in front of others, and always treated him as an eternal ally. A brother. Sully seemed to enjoy Jesse as someone outside his clique to use as an auxiliary wit for his own crusade.

Sully respected what he'd read of Jesse's writing. Jesse also exposed Sully to obscure songs, artists and books. Soon Jesse began to hear his own words, phrases and titles in Sully's songs.

The locals' interest in Jesse inspired some mysterious speculation. Jesse felt like an outsider in the downtown rock-and-roll circle as his presence conjured an inspired misunderstanding among them. A curiosity followed him through the cantinas. As the youngest member of this crowd, Jesse's exuberant literary intensity often alienated them.

As of late Jesse began to realize Sully basked in the security of his social appeal as a rock-and-roll persona among The Silvertones' fandom. Still, Jesse remained connected to Sully's dedication to craft. Sully signified Jesse's first friend that loved literature and music as much as himself. They'd lived almost four years in this old dilapidated apartment. Many late night indulgences revealed artistic intentions and worldly motivations sealing the friendship in sober, psychic and inebriated conversations.

Sully emerged from the bedroom with an empty plate that he disregarded without washing in the sink.

"What do you say we take our medicine?" asked Jesse. "I'll bring it out and you administer our dose, doctor."

He brought out the familiar mirror and a small bag of white crystals. Because of their shared intellectual pursuits, they found it fun to hang out alone with a large stash, play music and talk about their art or the stories of their heroes.

"You're not expecting company tonight, are you?" Jesse inquired.

"No. I told Annie not to fucking bring anyone over here tonight."

Jesse stood up and put a cassette of *The Basement Tapes* on the cheap stereo. He hovered over the mirror, lost in the ritual of chopping up the dust, cutting it into lines and preparing the bitter tasting powders.

Jesse crunched the small white rocks with a spoon. And then he chopped the dust into lines the width of a pencil almost four inches long. Jesse arranged the lines, and handed Sully the mirror for the customary first snort. Sully inhaled the dust through a plastic pen shaft cut in half. He stared at the blue and gold tapestry on the living room wall.

"Ol' Sam gave you a good deal," said Jesse.

"Yeah. It was a good batch today."

"His dealing is becoming too flagrant down at the bar. That ain't cool. He's totally lost his discretion."

"You speak the truth, my brother."

Jesse inhaled the second line, feeling the bitter powder crash against the back of his throat, swallowing the dust, burning and numbing everything down to his stomach. Even his bowels arranged to expel. Tell tale symptoms. Dryness. Sniffing. Adrenaline. The narcotic clarity awakens raw nerves.

"These local busts are getting serious," uttered Sully, preoccupied, pouring more dust onto the mirror.

"They are serious. Most of these people are amateurs. They just want everyone to know they're getting high. What they don't realize, just because they do drugs doesn't give them depth. I wrote poems and stories long before I did drugs, and you played guitar long before you did drugs. Intoxicants add an edge for a while, an element, but without style and practice that existed before the drugs, craftwise, there's no lasting creation. Too many people just don't understand that."

Jesse massaged his right nostril. They basked in mutual telepathy of the other's light.

"Drugs ain't really creative anyway," said Sully, sniffing a line and then inquiring, "hey, what did you and Felix talk about today?"

"Oh, well, shit. He told me Annie said I scored some tar from Sam. She doesn't need to say that."

"No, she doesn't."

"He jabbered about stealing somebody's stash, fucking up the guy, he even mentioned killing him, and he wanted me to help basically."

Sully looks up from the mirror momentarily to fix his dark brown eyes on Jesse, and then goes back to crunching powder on the mirror, "Strangeness. That guy makes me nervous."

"Yeah. Me, too."

It started getting late the drugs started getting low. Everything even conversation remained interesting as long as the drugs were in supply. The mojo dust gripped their minds. A mean desperation creeped upon them as dawn approached.

The nerve-shredding effects of the drug grinded on these friends as the sun began to come up. Paraphernalia on the kitchen table included a mirror, guitar picks, matches, a pipe, Jesse's notebooks, a tape recorder, candles, beer bottles, incense and a copy of Baudelaire's *Flowers of Evil*.

The sun would rise in less than an hour. A slow voice of ruin reminded Jesse as another working day arrived, they were already at leasteight hours behind on sleep. The bag was empty. Eyes shifted with nothing else to say.

"Well, hellfire. I'll see you tomorrow. I gotta try and sleep," moaned Sully, his eyes black holes of narcotic fatigue.

"Okay, ol' boy."

Sully closed the door to his bedroom. Jesse forced himself to lie in bed. He was unable to sleep. He wondered how long these circumstances could continue before imploding. His indulgence continually slowed progress on his work however, but an electric understanding existed between him and Sully, cementing the belief that they shared critical time together. But these days doubt began to creep in.

Chirping birds outside his window brought a desperate sigh from Jesse. He tossed and turned on the dirty sheets. He missed Sara. The loud trash truck arrived at seven o'clock to empty the huge metal disposal of the east wing in the apartment complex. The busy clamor of an early workday, the dust and a worried mind would not allow him to sleep until later that night.

4

When Felix called The Junk House phone an electronic voice informed him the number was temporarily disconnected. Felix decided he should try and find a ride to the Junk House to see what was going on.

He'd not spoken with anyone from there in several days. He watched Cook wave at him from a car yesterday with a grin on his face that revealed everything. The Cook never smiled.

Felix knew Fleshman remained wary of him. No matter how he tried he could not seem to act natural around Fleshman, and he understood Fleshman wasn't interested in being his friend.

Felix bought a pack of Marlboros. He ducked into The Neon Eel to hide from the cold. A television above the bar showed a basketball game. A redneck couple played pool and downtown regulars sat at the bar, but Felix didn't see anyone from the Junk House gang.

5

Broke again, he thought as this perpetual state of poverty heaved clarity upon his weary senses. The neglected rent stood past due two weeks ago, and this month's utility bills remained unpaid. Even his stash fell low.

Gray battalions of rain fell from the late January sky. Jesse ducked into The Neon Eel in search of someone owing him a drink. He knew payday arrived tomorrow. A damp chill lingered on his bones while the rainstorm droned some cosmic symphony. Another week burned to an end as Jesse realized his personal threads had rotted apart like a chaotic nightmare of wanton fate. He grew tired of rain.

The clock read four o'clock, yet the day seemed older under such an overcast light. The Neon Eel had only just opened. Upon entering the dim cantina, its overwhelming stench was disguised by a bleach scent that flooded one's senses.

Jesse removed his windbreaker. His blue jeans were damp, but his thermals remained warm. His feet felt webbed inside his cowhide boots. His brown unwashed hair matted against his skull. He felt as if he were fighting a cold. His blue eyes darkened without light from the sun. Doreen emerged from storing beer in the freezer. He knew he needed to dry out.

"Hey there, Jesse."

"Hey, Doreen."

"What's it gonna be?"

"Oh, I suppose the usual."

Doreen smiled and poured a glass of beer. She placed the glass in front of him on the wooden bar. She began cutting lemons and oranges for the bar fruit tray. Jesse dropped two dollars in the tip jar. Doreen never charged him for drinks.

"So what's going on?" asked Jesse.

"Same old shit. Dog got out of the pen last night. Spent the night chasing the fucker through the woods."

"Damn, did you catch her?"

"Hell yes, two hours later could've killed that damn dog."

"At least you caught her."

"I've got someone mending the fence today."

"Good deal. Hey, ya' seen Sam?"

"No, but I'm looking for his ass myself. He ran off with my money last night. You never know with Sam these days. Let me get this place set up first before Buck gets here and chews my ass for chatting. Damn, you looked soaked. Let me turn up the heat."

"It smells like a five hundred pound cat pissed in here."

"Buck keeps calling plumbers but can't none of 'em fix the damn toilet."

Drums of thunder rolled across the sky and shook the building like it meant to crack it open. Doreen toiled about doing her daily chores of unlocking the pool tables and cleaning glasses. Outside a random shard of lightning flashed in the distance like some omnipotent electric thread. Jesse realized he should be at home in front of the typewriter.

"Looks like this storm is here to stay for a while," Jesse said to Doreen, who toiled on the other side of the bar. He watched the silent big-screen television showing a horse race as the rain rolled in a light silver stream down the avenue. He perused the local arts newspaper. He noticed the neon bar sign in the window casting a strange electric beauty against a cold dark sky.

In some hallucinated recollection, Jesse replayed Sara's reaction after reading his first unpublished novel. "What do you mean it's fiction? Those scenes with her?" She scrutinized him with those sorrowful, deep blue eyes.

"Sara, they are only characters in a story."

"You don't really expect me to believe that, do you?"

"Listen, for the sake of telling a story with the intention of ripping the reader's heart out, especially if the writer has the gumption to create something that will endure long after he is dead. There has to be something at stake. Sometimes you have to weave elements from your own life into a story, or the seed to what inspires you to write it in the first place.

"Sometimes you make stuff up. We've talked about this before. An artist can't create anything he does not understand; he may not know how he went about creating such a thing, but he cannot create something he does not understand.

"It's just a story. Just because you know me, or a couple of my characters remind you of someone you or I know, or once knew, does not mean the story is about them or you, or any real person. They are characters-caricatures for the reader to identify with in his own life.

"Storytelling, like any other form of art, comes down to necessity and entertainment. You try to inspire and create a higher order of existence amid daily mundane events and bullshit everyone knows so well. The characters are only symbols existing for the story."

As Jesse sat at the bar waiting for Sam, he remembered tears welling in Sara's eyes. He missed her. He knew she did not understand any of this, very few did. There was no frame of reference for a writer's wife or lover who must suffer intolerable isolation, and poverty. A mortal blues.

Her reaction back then still stung him, "I find the analogy all too familiar. We're twenty-seven years old. You're not making any money this way. You never have to stop writing, but you have to work."

He knew she was right. He must get something going. If things continued along this path, they must separate, and he would likely end up as another downtown casualty. He felt for a long time a darkness abided within him from not cultivating his own gift.

The same dilemma threaded his days. Jesse worked at a telecommunications agency in the advertising department. He detested the job, and aimed to quit several times a week. He worked a makeshift schedule. Most of the money he earned originated from accounts he obtained years before, when he had just graduated from the university.

In the past week or so he had begun to funnel his energy into his craft. For quite some time he had scanned over outlines for his two unpublished novels, but he could get neither into a completed form. Jesse believed he was on the verge of a breakthrough with his writing.

Jesse saw his cheap rent and interesting companions as outweighing the liability of poverty and personal habits. He believed his time with Sully and the Junk House gang represented operating in the eye of the storm, which would allow him to write with a savage clarity.

As Jesse sipped his beer, Sam Tanner walked through the front door of The Neon Eel.

"Well, well, well."

"Good afternoon there, Jesse."

"Top of the day to you, Sam."

They shook hands and slapped each other on the back. Sam shook off the cold.

"Doreen, may I have a margarita please?"

"Not until you tell me what the hell happened to you last night."

"Darling, I was unavoidably detained. However, I do have something for you today."

Sam always reminded Jesse of a cross between the *Confederacy of Dunces* main character, Ignatius J. Reilly, and the guitarist Lowell George. A corpulent, moustached, goodnatured jokester, carpenter, musician, intellectual and drug addict. Sam Tanner, almost ten years older than Jesse, once operated as a road manager for another famous local rockandroll band, Gasoline Alley, and paved the way for The Silvertones years later. Sam now made a living as a sometime, carpenter and, as of late, drug dealer.

"Ya' want a bump?" Sam asked Jesse.

"Si senor."

"Follow me to my office. They walked into the men's bathroom and locked a stall. They found discretion in latrines for contraband indulgence. Sam pulled out a key and dipped it into a golfballsized bag of mojo dust. Sam held a gob of powder to Jesse's right nostril. Jesse inhaled. The same procedure continued in both nostrils for each man several times. Bitter powders swallowed in a sniff...

"Whew, thanks!" said Jesse, massaging his nose. A veil seemed lifted in his mind.

"I need to sell some of this. I gotta go. I'll be at the house in a couple of hours. Come on by and I'll watch out for you. Where's Sully?"

"At work."

"Meet me at my place around seven. We'll drink a bottle, and have a little dust."

"If that's cool."

"You're always welcome, Jesse."

"I appreciate that."

"I'll see you later."

"Adios."

Jesse returned to the bar. He felt refreshed, but the effects never lasted long enough. With the dust, an insatiable craving laced each fleeting sniff. Rare moments of insight still emerged for him by using the dust, but they were becoming few and far between these days. He left three dollars in the tip jar. He stood up.

"Bye, Doreen, I'll see ya' tomorrow."

"See ya' later, Jess"

6

At 7:15 p.m., Jesse knocked on the Junk House door. The old, one-story white dilapidated house, built in the late 1800s, earned its name serving as a reservoir for junkies, drunks and assorted other ne'er-do-wells. The house bordered on being condemned. A bonechilling wind whipped and howled while Jesse waited, shifting weight from one leg to the other. He watched his steaming breath.

Richard Fleshman, who lived at the Junk House, answered the door in a long, red nightshirt, resembling a young Uncle Scrooge. Fleshman, a year younger than Sam Tanner, looked at Jesse and said nothing. He left the door open, walked to a faded green couch and stretched out on it. Jesse walked inside, and closed the door behind him. The fireplace blazed a festive heat inside the living room.

"Sam here?"

"Not yet," responded Lane Lennear, another Junk House resident. "Have a seat. He'll be here in a minute."

A musty scent, like smoldering feet, or some other unkempt sour reeked throughout this humble dwelling. A painting by Lawson Miller, an old mutual friend of theirs who committed suicide, hung on the wall over the large, faded television playing at a volume rendering conversation unnecessary. Newspapers, crossword puzzles, science fiction books, ashtrays, empty beer cans, old pizza boxes, dirty dishes and soiled clothing lay scattered across the living room.

Jesse and Sully began keeping time with this crew several years ago as Sully's notoriety brought Jesse into the local rock-and-roll orbit. The Junk House gang were a little older and ran with a few of the local artists, like Gasoline Alley and the Silvertones, who brought the town international musical attention. They operated on the pulse of the town's artistic, hedonistic and contraband nexus.

With Sam and Sully missing at the moment Jesse felt uneasy in this company. He sat next to the fire. Richard Fleshman had long made it evident he did not really like Jessehis occasional lethal jest and drunken insult smeared any conversation or encounter. Fleshman had never given reason for his open hostility. He sat on the couch playing with his ponytail without ever looking at Jesse.

Lane Lennear, a gray-haired fellow wearing wire-rimmed glasses who reminded Jesse of a college professor, sat reading on the couch. The fourth Junk House resident the one they called the Cook relaxed on the couch that was considered his bed. It was a three-bedroom house. Cook sought refuge in recipes, historic battles and narcotics.

Felix sat at the coffee table beside Fleshman. As the only other non-resident, Felix never seemed to make eye contact with anyone. This harlequin assemblage thrived on a constant party atmosphere existing around the four men living at this ramshackle abode, not to mention the peripheral friends who spent many evenings here.

Each of the Junk House member's ages neared forty, leaving Jesse and Sully as the youngest members of the gang. Just as Jesse picked up the Sunday edition of the Atlanta Constitution, the front door opened and Sam Tanner walked into the living room bringing cold air from the outside in with him. Steam smoked from his mouth as he removed a torn and frayed blue ski jacket.

"Evening, girls."

Some laughed, while others muttered greetings.

Felix spoke in strained attention, "It's about time."

"I don't know why you'd be waiting on me," Sam replied to Felix and then sat at the old, oak table across from Jesse.

"Cook, what you been doin' all night? Lying around drinking my beers, watching TV all fucking night?" Sam inquired.

"Hey, fuck you son of a bitch. There's beef stew in the kitchen."

"Yeah, your famous radioactive beef stew."

Empty beer cans lay in idle disregard marking where a drinker once sat. Fleshman opened the front door to blow away Sam's intestinal effluvium. Sam produced a small bag from his pocket.

"Hand me that mirror," Sam said to Jesse, and sat down to chop the bitter mojo dust.

"Shut that fucking door," barked Sam. Fleshman closed the door without a word. Fleshman looked at Jesse in a way that said to him, "Why are you here? You're not welcome."

Sam crushed the dust into six lines. For six takers. No one spoke during this anticipated ritual in fleeting pleasures of the flesh. Sam said to no one in particular: "You fuckers are gonna owe me some money for this."

The roommates gazed at one another, weighing distribution of wealth among them. A straw passed between them for several turns, common to such indulging rituals. The dust created a certain narcotic clarity making conversation flow easier. A new energy…

"Cook, I bet you didn't save me any of those Valiums, did you?"

"Sam, you faithless ass." The Cook stood up and disappeared into the kitchen. He emerged and laid four blue pills on the table in front of Sam.

"Well, thank you, honey."

The high ceiling dangled a broken fan. Worn couches and duct-taped cushions soon served as instruments of comfort. A Rockford Files rerun played on the faded television screen. Sam commenced to chopping twelve more lines.

"They say the cops are squeezing for a bust," stated Felix.

"When are they not squeezing?" sneered Fleshman with a sniff.

"Some sort of sting operation. You can usually feel it coming."

"If you could feel it coming, you wouldn't get busted, would you?"

Jesse watched Sam chopping the lines, trying to ignore the tension shifting in the air.

"Getcha' drink, Jesse," offered the Cook, handing Jesse a bottle of Old Granddad. Jesse consented, rifling the burning whiskey down his throat. His stomach turned. His teeth gnashed. He wiped his mouth on his flannel sleeve.

The mirror came around the table and landed in front of Jesse. The powder for him remained as an extravagance but wasn't his preferred vice. The potent dust gagged him when he snorted it.

"Hey man, did the *Four Corner* ever run one of those stories you submitted?" Sam randomly asked Jesse while the others talked about another episode of the Rockford Files.

"Fuck no. They're too hip for me."

"That shit they print sucks. They never publish anything worth a shit, so you must be on the right track...run me off copies of those couple stories you showed me a few weeks ago."

"I can do that."

Jesse knew he wouldn't see Sara until the weekend.

Since Sully departed for work the Junk House cured Jesse's loneliness today even though he knew he should be writing.

He always tried to funnel the druginduced energy into some creative vortex. Yet, Jesse knew an over indulgence in the powders killed his creativity. His clarity evaporated as he struggled to maintain an equilibrium of selfexpectation and selfrealization with anxiety.

"Damn, Cook, take a fucking shower every now and then would you?"

"Fuck you, Fleshman...you fucking woman beater..."

"Hey...hey," soothed Sam.

Jesse ignored this domestic reference and indulged in another line set aside in his name. Then he surrendered the straw to the Cook who peered over Jesse's shoulder, pressing for a turn with tunnel vision. As Jesse turned to notice what flickered on the television, he heard Lennear shout: "What the fuck!" Lennear glared at the Cook.

"Oh, sorry, Lane," the Cook stuttered, sniffing, satisfied with a fiendish smile, sauntering away, as if he forgot his restriction to participate in this turn.

"You fucking asshole."

"I just lost m'self, Lane, sorry."

They all watched, allowing the situation to diffuse itself. Felix laughed in the corner, stewing in great pleasure at this domestic confrontation.

"What the fuck is so funny?" asked Fleshman, staring at Felix with beady eyes.

"Fuck you, Fleshman, don't start."

Fleshman became insulted at Felix's nonchalance. His eyes burned like two hot marbles and said,

"Fuck me? Fuck you, cocksucker. I live here."

As Jesse raised his beer to drink, Fleshman crossed the room and began strangling Felix. Chairs were overturned. Sam got up, protecting the mirror, placing it upon the mantle above the fireplace, and helped pull Felix off Fleshman, who had a blue vein bulging in his forehead the size of a pencil.

Cook and Lennear struggled to keep the two separated. Felix looked unsettled, but not completely surprised by Fleshman's action.

"You're gonna do that one too many times, Fleshman!" Felix screamed with a yellow glare, struggling to break free from Lennear. Felix weighed about two hundred pounds.

"Fuck you! I don't know why you come around here anyway. Get out of my fucking house! Get out!"

Felix snatched himself from Lennear's weak grip, exiting the Junk House, and slammed the front door behind him. A perverse tension hung throughout the room as glances were exchanged.

"I'm sick of that motherfucker!" shouted Fleshman. Sam replaced the table and chairs in their proper place like nothing happened. They sat down and took a few deep breaths. Sam retrieved the mirror. He chopped five thick lines. When the mirror was passed to him, Jesse indulged.

...

After Felix departed, Lennear and Sam began pestering Cook for a drug to calm them down after all the powder they inhaled. For the last few weeks, they waited anxiously for their portion of the rare contraband Cook obtained from his secret connection the day before.

Cook worked with an individual whose roommate was employed at a pharmaceutical warehouse. Cook's source supplied him with various amounts of zombie dust and rare pharmaceuticals at specific times and different locations. Cook kept silent about how much and when he scored.

Through the years Cook kept the same connection, yet he never revealed the main source, not even to his closest friends. He made sure all transactions remained untraceable. Sometimes he'd make a purchase from a known dealer to throw off the scent of his friends and anyone else interested in his black market activities. Cook maintained a code of secrecy with his supplier on all levels, at all costs.

"So you gonna break out the goodies?"

Sam inquired. "Yeah, I am. Turn the heat up in this joint. Feels like a fucking meat locker in here."

The Cook collected money from each roommate toward this volume purchase. In their inebriated state and fresh off the confrontation between Fleshman and Felix, the Junk House, quartet with Cook leading, began their regular narcotic ritual forgetting that an outsider, Jesse, was present. This was the only time they had let their guard down in this regard.

Lucky for them, Jesse was too high to notice the Cook's role in their dealing machine. Sam was the only publicly known Junk House resident who dealt with buyers and he would have to make up the money he paid out to Cook by selling parts of his score to others.

Cook sat down at the table, brushing aside old newspapers and stray papers. He grabbed the house mirror and produced the drugs.

The Cook held the package as everyone waited to taste the rare dust. He opened it and pulled out a motley assemblage of pills packed in individual bags.

"Hmmm. Percocet. Codeine. Lorcet. Demerol. I don't know what these e-e-evillooking green ones are." Cook held the pill up to the light inspecting it with a close scrutiny.

"There you go, Jesse, ten Percocet, seven Lortab, and three bonus Demerols for picking my friend up last week."

"Damn, thanks Cook." Jesse always enjoyed prescription pain-killers because there was never a question of their effectiveness.

"Will somebody turn up the fucking heat!" said Cook again as he spilled a fair amount of very light brown zombie powder onto the house mirror. He began dividing the powder with care.

"How you gonna do it?" asked Fleshman.

"I wish we could shoot it," replied the Cook. "Shoot mojo dust?" asked Jesse, dropping the pill in his shirt pocket.

"No, zombie powder," responded Cook.

Jesse's eyebrows raised and he leaned closer to the mirror, inspecting the rare, highly addictive and dangerous powder, then said: "You could snort it off a toothpick."

"We'll just line it up," said Cook.

Fine lines of zombie powder sat divided on the mirror. Everyone sniffed one small line. Only Sam drank beer. Cook cut another round of lines once everyone gathered around the table. The room temperature increased both from the door being shut and the manifesting effects of the drugs. Jesse became so comfortable he removed his boots. He felt a thick, warm euphoria ease his senses, realizing there's nothing like high-grade black market anesthesia. Jesse's face began to itch. He could feel a slow, natural twisting of his stomach. He experienced a fluttering in his ears.

Lennear rushed to the bathroom. Fleshman stumbled outside. They vomited from the dosage. Sam strummed his acoustic guitar with a slow, delicate tone. Cook flicked channels on the television.

"Where's Sully?" Sam asked Jesse.

"He's at work tonight," murmured Jesse as if someone spoke to him in a dream.

Lennear returned to the table slackjawed and red eyed. The Cook walked into the dank bathroom. They heard him lock the door. Jesse got up, opened the front door, walked outside and vomited behind a row of boxwood trees. The regurgitation didn't resemble a drunk sick, but a natural processnot gut wrenching, but certainly an inconvenience. Stomach contents spilled out. The fluttering in his ears persisted.

Jesse felt as if his bones liquefied. When he walked back inside and sat down on the couch, his foot felt sticky. He thought he probably threw up on himself, but when he looked down he noticed a blood stained sock on his left foot. He had stepped on a broken whiskey bottle while vomiting.

"Fuck," Jesse uttered, pulling off his blood stained sock.

"What happened to you?" asked Sam, noticing Jesse's bloody sock.

"Stepped on some broken glass would've cut my fucking toe off and never known it," he mumbled and winced, realizing the wound should be painful even though he was numb. Blood dripped from the long toe, next to the big one.

"I didn't have time to put on my boots or I would've puked on your carpet. Good thing I'm stoned."

"We have the best medicine in the world, but you should always wear shoes around this place. I'll get you something to put on that." Sam disappeared into the kitchen. He returned with iodine, bandages, cotton balls and a bright yellow sock.

"The sock ain't pretty but it's clean. It's never been worn." Sam set the items on the table in front of Jesse, who stared at his bloody wound with a strange fascination.

"Is it bad?" asked Lennear in a low, distant concern.

"I don't think so." Jesse dabbed at the wound with a cotton ball and iodine and he slowly managed to apply a large Band Aid. After staring at his wounded toe for several minutes, he put on the bright yellow sock.

"What the fuck is Cook doing? It seems like he's been in the bathroom six fucking hours," said Fleshman, who started banging on the bathroom door.

"You better not be doing any of that powder in there!"

Sam noticed the dust vial wasn't on the mirror. "How long's he been in there?" asked Fleshman. "I can't tell," responded Lennear.

"About ten minutes I think," Jesse muttered from the couch without looking up from his wound.

"What the fuck." Fleshman pounded on the door. It was locked.

"Open the fucking door!" screamed Fleshman. Even in his drug-induced state, Sam envisioned Cook snorting the remaining stash in the bathroom. Fleshman held his ear to the door listening for movements on the other side. Sam returned from his bedroom with a devoid credit card. He fiddled with the lock a few seconds until the door opened. Cook rested unconscious on the bathroom floor with his feet in the bathtub.

"Oh, Jesus," Lennear muttered.

"You stupid son of a bitch," said Fleshman, as he began splashing water from the sink onto the Cook's face.

"His lips ain't blue and he's still breathing. Where's the stash?" Sam Tanner asked in a voice he did not recognize as his own. Fleshman slapped the Cook while Sam picked the vial on the back of the toilet. He noticed the contents in the vial seemed untouched.

"It's from those pills he eats-not the powder," speculated Fleshman.

"I had a feeling this was gonna happen," wheezed Lennear.

"Then why did you let it happen, you fucking moron!"

"Fuck you, Fleshman-I have no control over him."

"You guys shut the fuck up!" yelled Sam. It was the most serious Jesse had ever seen him. Sam's thick face turned crimson red.

"I have some mojo dust, and it'll wake him up, but I'm getting tired of bailing him out when he fucks up."

Fleshman and Lennear sat the barely conscious Cook in a chair at the table. He rested there like some devoid Frankenstein.

"Cook, wake up you dumb ass, snort this dust." The suddenly lucid Cook accepted the rolled dollar bill and with innate precision, inhaled a line of mojo dust.

"Nothing like a little speedball," the Cook muttered, passing the bill to Sam.

"Yeah, well, I'm tired of you wiggin' out doin' all our drugs," said Fleshman.

"Fuck you, Fleshman, if it weren't for me, you wouldn't be able to sleep."

Sam sat surprised at the Cook's current clarity. A strange silence hung in the air. They all forgot about Jesse sitting on the couch with a bloody sock near him on the floor. Just then there was a knock at the door.

Fleshman tiptoed to the door. He peeped through the sight hole and said: "It's Nancy."

"Let her in," said Sam.

Nancy Mulberry, an old friend of the gang, owned The Blue Bistro, an upscale restaurant in town. She watched out for the gang as well as she could. They joked and called her a nag because she often warned them to keep their waywardness in control.

Nancy was an attractive thirty-five year old woman. Her dark ringlets of hair fell to her shoulders. Her dark eyebrows arched over her brown walnut eyes. Her voluptuous figure distracted men. Today she wore overalls. She often suffered teasing from the guys because of her beauty.

Nancy first noticed Jesse's hands stained with what looked like his own blood. She'd seen him out in the bars drinking downtown, and thought him attractive, but she didn't know him. She sensed some symbolic mischief occurred here this evening. The Cook stood up from the table and sneered at her like some invalid Lazarus returned from the tomb.

They all looked whacked out of their minds, and yet a vague tension circulated she couldn't pinpoint; but of course, it was the contrary Mr. Fleshman who addressed her first.

"Hey, Nancy, you're only ten minutes late. Cook almost overdosed."

"You're kidding me." She placed her hands on her chest in a stricken manner. Then she noticed fresh urine stains on the army pants Cook wore. Nancy said nothing at first, understanding where the tension came from, and then she looked at Jesse.

"What's wrong with him?"

"He cut his foot on some glass," answered Lennear, watching his cigarette smoke drift toward the ceiling. The Cook sang to himself with his eyes closed.

"This is insane. Every time I come over here you guys are trying to kill yourselves. It's the same scene every night. Fights or some other intoxication problem is going on. Why don't you just go out and buy a gun and blow your fucking heads off!"

Fleshman began chopping the powders. He casually spoke to Sam. "We might as well speedball the rest."

"Yes, yes, speedballs," mumbled the Cook.

"You're not listening to me!" cried Nancy.

At that moment Jesse noticed Nancy. He saw her as some beautiful messenger.

"You're telling me he almost overdosed, and you're chopping him more lines?"

"It'll make his heart beat faster, Nancy. Now ease up. It's not the time for one of your motherly lectures."

"No, it's never fucking time." The lines in her face seemed to disappear. "When are you guys going to wise up? Sam, don't laugh. You've lost everything for an excuse of being a drunk and a drug addicta wife, a kid. Richard, you're the same."

Fleshman sniffed two lines then pushed the mirror toward Sam, who sniffed, and in turn Lennear, Jesse, and finally the Cook.

"Are you listening to me?"

"Nancy. Calm down. Cook is still breathing, if you'll notice, he's vacuuming up all my dust," said Sam in a soothing tone.

"This isn't funny. It's ridiculous. Nothing lasts forever. You guys always crave change, well, it's coming. And I got a bad feeling."

Her face lost all expression, as if she summed everything up for them, and in the process reaffirmed the truth for herself. Fleshman became annoyed.

"This is fucking ridiculous. Don't come in here."

"Oh yeah, go into the old routine of getting pissed off. I've seen it all before."

"We just want to prove we can kill ourselves before life does it to us," Fleshman responded.

"Great. That's genius, Fleshman. Very inspired perspective, but it has absolutely nothing to do with anything. I'm no babysitter. I'll see you guys later." She picked up her purse and keys.

"But, Mom!" cajoled Fleshman, but Nancy already slammed the door and was gone.

"I love that girl," said Sam sincerely. "Cut out one more."

A blissful lethargy crept upon them dilated eyes, itching, unctuous flesh. The dust became low. Jesse did not want to wear out his welcome since he contributed no money toward the stash.

"Fellas, thanks for the buzz. I'm gonna head out while I'm still conscious." Jesse held his boot in his hand and hobbled toward the door.

"Okay, ol' boy."

"Have a good night."

"Take care."

Jesse could only walk on the heel of his injured foot. He closed the Junk House door with quiet tact. Outside, the cold air felt good. Steam smoked from his mouth. He hobbled across Jupiter Street, feeling a sense of profound consequence along this wayward path leading to his front door. He remembered the pills in his pocket. He felt his spirit clawing at his mind.

Damp winds chilled him as he smelled wood smoke floating in the air on this perfect tranquil evening. A biblical mist smothered these rolling hills in a melodious utterance of some forgotten backwoods rhapsody. Dead leaves scattered and swirled down the street in the wind. Jesse closed and locked his door. He rested on the bed before he soon nodded out. Demons danced to a symphony in his head. Somewhere between a memory and a dream Jesse sensed a hellhound sniffing outside his door...something evil lurked...waiting for the precise moment to descend.

On Friday, a quiet, gray afternoon mist hovered over the ground. The rain approached for this shiftless season. For two months tonight's soldout gig served as a source of anticipation. Tonight Sully served as the opening act for the Silvertones, whose new album release performance would be broadcast live on the radio. The Silvertones were now a profitable rockandroll business. They weren't a hometown band anymore.

Rain droned over their decrepit apartment building. When Jesse opened his bedroom door, Sully already sat at the kitchen table, changing strings on his Telecaster guitar. Silver wires lay scattered all around his chair.

"You're up early."

"Yeah, I wanted to get some strings."

"You walked downtown in the rain?"

"I got lucky. It wasn't raining."

"Hell, I could've driven you down."

"Don't sweat it."

Opening up for the Silvertones this evening would expose Sully to various record labels and industry people. Among locals, it was no secret Sully existed on the verge of mainstream success. Strangers often approached Sully acting like some long lost friend. The phone rang more these days. Jesse almost never answered letting the answering machine pick up. Now vultures loomed to share Sully's ride, wedging their illweaved ambition into his personal operation promising that their presence would make a difference.

Jesse found it more difficult to work here at the apartment. The place once served as a very productive lair where he retreated from familiar friends to write, but these days the place never retained privacy. The vultures showed up here for action at any time of the day or night to warm their hands around Sully's creative fire.

"Will there be any medicine tonight?" Jesse heard himself ask, gathering a towel for a shower.

"It shouldn't be a problem. Skinny's gonna watch out for us."

"Are you playing with Eddie and Vern tonight?"

"I'll call." Sully paused and added, "If they're available and sober enough."

"Well let me know about the stash. I'll go in half with you."

"No problem."

Jesse heard the phone ringing as he climbed into the shower. Then he heard Sully say, "Hey Annie."

As Jesse pulled on his boots, he could hear Sully tuning his guitar. Jesse smoked his pipe. He walked into the kitchen and made a strong drink of bourbon and coke.

...

Sully acted unusually quiet before the show. After they finished their drinks, Jesse drove Sully down with his guitars and amplifier to The Rain Palace, a fifteen-hundred seat theatre. Sully seemed distant.

Lately, Jesse noted a vague tension existing between them.

Sully dressed in the same clothes he had worn all week adhering to his usual indifference. His cigarette smoke clouded Jesse's truck. The damp conditions were soaking everything.

The Silvertones' tour bus sat parked outside the theatre when Jesse drove into the parking lot. Their tour commenced next weekend in Charlotte, North Carolina. Jesse watched as members of the Silvertones' road crew assembled equipment for the evening's show-rolling amplifiers, drums and other music equipment up a ramp leading into the building.

As they got out of the truck, a slashing wind came across them. Low overcast clouds cast dark shadows on the day. A strange excitement circulated around town, as if holidays were approaching. Local music critics and intelligentsia would be out tonight for the Silvertones' live broadcast performance. The theatre's neon lights seemed brighter against the overcast sky.

"Sully!" The band's road crew all howled with gracious greetings.

"Hey boys!"

These long-haired, bearded young men wearing flannel shirts, blue jeans and boots smiled upon seeing Sully.

They assured him his equipment would be assembled for him this evening.

"Y'all know Jesse," said Sully motioning to Jesse, who shook hands with everyone.

They walked into the empty theatre from a side door. Jesse enjoyed being in the bars and theatres during the day, while the places remained empty and quiet with only a few employees and musicians wandering around during soundcheck. The Rain Palace's old Moroccan architecture offered a colorful ceiling hovering over the stage. A scent of varnish lingered in the air.

When evening descends, though Jesse realized how the old building transforms into something opposite of innocent. As of now, a daytime business-like normalcy circulated around these musical proceedings. A fan would never guess local legends prowled the grounds.

Sully discovered the Silvertones bestowed him with his own dressing room and ice chest full of Budweiser. Jesse overheard Sully say to Skinny Bartlett, the Silvertones' road manager, "We need to score."

They stood in the Silvertones' dressing room. The wine colored carpet with intricate gold designs lined the floors. Mirrors covered the dressing room walls.

"Scoring is no problem," Skinny, the dangerously thin, crewcut road manager replied, as he twisted an allaccess plastic laminate hanging around his neck. Sully and Skinny disappeared out the back door, onto the tour bus for a few minutes. Jesse read the local arts newspaper until Sully returned.

"I got a whole bag of the zombie and mojo," whispered Sully, giving the small packages to Jesse for safe-keeping. Then he left to sound check his instruments.

Sully played songs only Jesse heard him play around the house. No one else heard these songs. Sully always kept the sound checks interesting. He joked with various Silvertones management people.

Jesse thought of Sara. He missed her. He knew they were falling apart. Where was all this getting him? He realized he should be at home writing and revising, but distractions lingered at hand. He noticed various locals milling outside the theatre looking for someone they knew who could get them tickets into this sold out affair.

While Jesse sat drinking a Budweiser and refocusing on Sully's playing, he noticed Silvertones' drummer, Big Jim Turner, ushering Sam Tanner and Felix in the dressing room back door. They did not notice Jesse.

Sully played a Jimmie Rodgers song. Satisfied with the sound, he unplugged his guitar from the amplifier, dropped his brass slide in his pocket and told the road crew he'd see them later. They walked down the stage steps and Sully said to Jesse knowing it would be a couple of hours before showtime: "Let's head back to the house." In the truck they rode anxious to get into the stash Skinny had provided Sully.

"Did you get a gram of both?"

"Yeah."

"That should do it."

"I'm gonna take it easy until I finish playing."

Jesse understood the preshow protocol. Sully enjoyed constructing a secretive veil around himself, keeping his creative persona impenetrable. He and Jesse shared this "behind the curtain" code. Even when he felt this code seemed to fuel his friend's vanity, Jesse ignored it for the sake of the craft. He saw this as continuing evidence of how each gravitated toward the other's conviction.

Tonight Sully composed part of the town's main attraction, and Jesse recognized how the local importance inflated Sully's ego. Through small acts he'd remind Jesse this was his zone, his arena or his element. He had always enjoyed the local admiration and curiosity he received from the Silvertones' fans, but Jesse began to wonder if Sully as capable of burning friendships for the sake of fame or fortune.

They drove home in silence. Jesse felt he understood the crux of Sully's dilemma. Jesse saw the mass audiences of mainstream music fans as vultures. They sat in the shadows waiting for MTV, famous magazines or the news media at large to spoonfeed them their approved talents and geniuses.

Yet, on the other hand, Sully used Jesse's ideas without ever acknowledging their originator. Jesse was uncomfortable with both sides of the eerie reality.

The rain cleared while the day was not quite dark. They got out of the truck and entered their apartment. Jesse sat down at the cheap metal frame kitchen table and pulled two small plastic bags filled with bitter powder from an inside coat pocket.

"Should we do one?" asked Jesse.

"I'll do a couple mojos, but no zombie powder until after I play."

"I might just do one."

"Yeah. Me, too." Sully grinned, unable to refuse such a rare temptation. He laid the mirror in front of Jesse, who chopped the fine powders. Jesse lit a cinnamon candle to disguise the Middle Eastern cooking scent rising from the downstairs apartment. He remembered he hadn't eaten since yesterday's black bean burrito.

They sniffed the powders. Jesse always appreciated that no matter how fucked up or high Sully became, he never missed a show. It seemed to Jesse that Sully played just as good no matter how stoned or how sober he really was at the moment. Jesse thought again of how these music aficionados could not appreciate the difficulty of the craft, or the songwriting, much less performing while intoxicated or emotionally distraught.

"You should play 'Dead Flowers' tonight," Jesse suggested, sniffing one line of zombie powder and mojo dust. A speedball.

"Yeah. It's a good night for it," Sully muttered, taking the rolled up ten-dollar bill, and sniffed his two lines.

After a couple of hours, they called a taxi for the ride back downtown. Neither wanted to drive home intoxicated and holding contraband. The old cab driver smelled like whiskey. They didn't talk in the taxi.

When the cab pulled up to The Rain Palace, the grayheaded taxi driver with a reddish beard said to Jesse, who handed him the fare, "I knew you boys looked like rock and rollers, or some other sort of criminals like that."

...

The dim, mosque-like theatre glowed, possessing a life of its own once evening descended. A smoldering intensity permeated the atmosphere since this event had occupied local music aficionados conversations for weeks.

Jesse never envied Sully's preshow wait. They walked backstage, and upon entering the VIP room they realized the backstage area had transformed since this afternoon. Jesse noticed three catered buffet tables covered with wine, chicken, soft drinks, fruit, chips, chocolates, potato salad, cole slaw, assorted vegetables, pilaf, deli meats, coffee, vodka, scotch, whiskey, bottled water, bar pretzels, stray vegetables and various dips lined the dressing room. Jesse admired the buffet table, and walked past it.

Jesse heard Annie before he saw her. She stormed into the tuning room door. "Oh, who gives a fuck, Skinny! You know me! What do you think? I'm gonna go ask Sully for an autograph?" Annie's entrances were always loud and dramatic. This evening Doreen accompanied Annie.

"Hey there, Jesse!" said Doreen, giving him a hug.

"Hey, Doreen." A genuine affection existed between the two of them. Annie did not speak to Jesse as she walked past him looking for Sully. Once Annie was out of sight, Doreen asked Jesse, "Do you want a bump?"

"Sure."

They walked into the private dressing room where a small table sat in front of a full length mirror. They closed and locked the door. Doreen poured a little mojo dust into a pile on top of a fashion magazine. Just then, a disturbing knock at the dressing room door startled them. Jesse's first instinct told him it was Annie. He opened the door and peeked out to see Sam Tanner, Felix and Silvertones drummer Jim Turner. Jesse let them in.

Time seemed to accelerate as Jesse felt the anticipation for the evening's events peaking. Many folks walked around with glazed and wondrous looks in their eyes. Jesse imagined what Silvertones fans might give to change positions with him. Everyone in the dressing room snorted another two lines.

Once they all sniffed a turn, Jesse stood up to leave. He didn't want to wear out his welcome or seem to Jim Turner that he was clinging to stardom as Jesse assumed Felix was doing.

Such people with no talent figure the quickest way to greatness is riding the coattails of stars. Felix was talking nonstop, and the powder made Jesse intolerant of his jabbering.

"Well, I'll see y'all in a while," said Jesse, bidding adieu and gently closing the door. Just outside the office, at the end of the hall, Annie and Sully stood close to each other, apparently having a very private conversation. When Annie noticed Jesse walking up the hall, she said in a loud, sarcastic tone so all the Silvertones wives and crew could hear her challenging him with a snickering insult: "Here comes your number one fan!"

Neither Jesse nor Sully responded to Annie. Jesse knew she would never understand their relationship, but he cringed imagining what she said behind his back. As her relationship with Sully grew, Jesse's distrust and dislike of Annie mounted.

Her lethal jests painted him into a corner. If he was mean to her, he couldn't take a joke, but if he let it go, it encouraged such behavior. It seemed like she hated him.

Jesse saw Crazy Annie as a parasite. He never understood what Sully saw in her, besides her procuring him drugs. She was a whore for narcotic contraband, who only wanted to be known as Sully's girlfriend. Jesse knew that anyone who spent longer than one or two evenings with her had to recognize this savage fact. Yet, out of a sense of respect for his friend, Jesse kept his mouth shut.

Annie also made sure to get in with the wives of some of the Silvertones. Somehow she wedged her way into the circle of local artists. She seemed determined to sabotage Jesse's friendship with Sully, and it confused and hurt him.

Even though Sully and Annie fought constantly, Jesse recently felt Sully being drawn to Annie's side of the fence. A morbid intuition dogged Jesse and had him worried those closest to him were on the verge of selling him out or at the very least refusing to believe in him. He felt like a prisoner of their inspired misunderstandings with no way to convince them otherwise.

Sara often expressed certain misgivings to Jesse about these people. It reached a point that she wasn't interested in spending time with people who doubted, stole and insulted him. This was one of the main reasons that she never visited Jesse.

In this moment, Jesse missed Sara deeply. Yet, he also remembered the time she expressed little faith in his aspiration as a writer. He was caught between two worlds. Jesse became anxious. The powder distracted him. He went out to the concession area and bought an overpriced beer. He wanted Sully's show to be over with so they could leave this scene.

It made him feel worse to be here tonight. The fun was gone. He stood and sipped his beer, watching all these people blindly following along a generation of brain-damaged show offs. Jesse felt uneasy in this crowd of idolaters who needed other people to live their lives for them. They just wanted to be part of something. They wanted to get some fairy dust sprinkled on them by keeping close proximity to artists.

It reminded Jesse of an old Hemingway quote about warming their hands around the fire of artists: "They are nearly all loafers expending the energy that an artist puts into his creative work talking about what they are going to do and condemning the work of all artists who have gained recognition."

Jesse saw a merciless culture set up to honor the entertainers, athletes and the rich not the firemen, the nurses, the farmers or the hardworking people with real responsibilities in society like his parents who were teachers. Yet, Jesse respected the musicians and there could be no denying this evening lurked as the musical big timea traveling rock-and-roll show tonight on a live worldwide broadcast. The musicians spent years cultivating their craftlong before they were paid or earned attention from it.

Reluctantly, Jesse wandered toward the backstage entrance only to find radio and promotion people loitering. Jesse never cared much for the Silvertones' music, but because he saw them and their friends and family often, and they recorded several of Sully's songs, it became hard for Jesse not to like them and respect their accomplishments.

"Hey, Jesse!" He was surprised to hear his name called. He turned around and noticed two beautiful girls smiling at him. He'd seen only one of the girls before. The tall girl named Avalina, the very striking girl with long blonde hair, dark blue eyes and full scarlet lips. She wore a navy blue sweater and faded jeans that distracted him. He had met her several weeks before at a restaurant.

"You two are certainly a sight for sore eyes," Jesse said, hugging Avalina. She smelled like lavender. Her eyes were dilated.

"We noticed you were all alone. This is my friend Cindy. She's visiting from Charleston."

He shook hands with Cindy, a striking brown-haired girl with beautiful hazel eyes, smooth skin and who wore a very short miniskirt that displayed her perfectly sculptured legs. They watched Jesse. He did not want to believe what her revealing eyes told him. Telling glances.

"What are you girls up to tonight? Trouble? Y'all both look stunning."

"Not us. No trouble. No, sir."

"Cindy's a photographer. Why don't you take our picture?" Avalina put her arms around Jesse, and Cindy pulled out a Minolta camera and snapped two pictures of them.

"I'd like to get a copy of this photo," he said. "No problem, honey." Jesse realized if it wasn't for Sara, he'd pursue either of them. Although he remained faithful to Sara, these young hippy girls often tempted him. Avalina made it increasingly difficult for him to resist her. Doreen told him weeks ago that Avalina dated the Silvertones' guitar player, but she often dropped amorous hints toward Jesse. If she sat close to him, a part of her body always touched him.

Perhaps she found him extremely appealing because he had a girlfriend. Maybe Avalina sensed he wasn't chasing her. He once read married men put off pheromones that attract women. He wasn't married to Sara, but perhaps the same rules applied. Still, Avalina always acted very respectful toward him. At times he could hardly hear her soft voice when she spoke. She was only twenty-one after all.

"Jesse, I must say, as always, you're so handsome tonight. Look how blue his eyes are, Cindy."

"They are blue as yours. He is cute."

"I like that you're letting your hair grow out." Avalina playfully tugged at his locks.

"You're embarrassing me," he said, making the girls giggle.

The girls wore backstage laminates. Jesse didn't have one of those, but for some reason, no one ever questioned him. He figured he must look like he belonged here.

"Will you walk backstage with us?" Avalina asked, her arm still around his waist, her opulent eyes staring into his.

"Avalina, I'll go wherever you want me to go."

Jesse noticed fans watching them, wishing they had access to the Silvertones backstage area. Heads turned as the young trio walked through security. Soon all sorts of people enveloped these beautiful girls. Jesse left them in the VIP room. He then noticed Sully emerging from the restroom. Jesse wrote in his notebook to stay focused while he made notes regarding the evening's proceedings.

"Hey, lets step back in the office one more time," said Sully, referring to the maddening ritual. It was almost showtime. Jesse never envied the preshow wait. They performed the clandestine ritual with the mojo dust. Sully sat quiet. Jesse grabbed a bottle of water out of the cooler.

The Silvertones and their road crew grinned when Sully and Jesse emerged from the office, sniffing and rubbing their noses. They looked like a pair of mischievous brothers a great wanted outlaw poster.

Showtime arrived for Sully. The theatre lights dimmed. Jesse hid behind stacks of the Silvertones' Marshall amplifiers that were not in use for this solo performance. He had watched Sully play hundreds of gigs in empty dank taverns, and now this was an authentic music scene that could support itself.

Tonight stood out as a singular evening. The crowd stirred. Microphones littered the tapers' section. Without saying a word, Sully ripped into his song called "The Midnight Lamp," bringing the fat brass slide over his National Steel guitar. He sang looking out over the crowd, seeing nothing in particular.

The crowd cheered and clapped, but after the first few songs they grew anxious for the Silvertones. Sully possessed his share of devoted fans and some shouted out requests between songs. Most of his friends, though, thought he should already be "famous" by now. Sully did not smile or talk much between songs since he and Jesse had discussed proper onstage etiquette on many a night.

Jesse sneaked a look at the crowd. Some danced. Some stared. Jesse thought to himself how a moment always arises when the real spectacle bores the average viewer. Or when the willing suspension of disbelief fades. The dullness of reality sets in. The audience loses interest because anticipation often remains stronger than the event.

Jesse noticed activity picked up backstage. Radio people, management and club staff made him want to retreat into Sully's dressing room to wait. He knew for many of these people, the music wasn't the most important thing; the event was yet another reason to party.

Jesse understood that the music remained as a reason for people to get together but in the middle of the communal body, the music-although it remained a constant threadbecomes almost an inconvenience, secondary to drugs, money, conversations and hanging out. Jesse watched the continuing American tradition of rock-and-roll stardom unfolding before his eyes tonight.

He decided to fetch a beer, but he noticed Annie down the hallway talking to Jim Turner's wife, so Jesse decided to remain in his place behind the amplifiers. Sully played "Dead Flowers," which drew the loudest applause during his set. Jesse felt proud of Sully, like a brother done good.

Two songs later and with Annie out of view, Jesse walked toward the hallways and offices. He noticed Sam Tanner inviting people in and out of the office. Jesse saw the Ellis Brothers, Vern & Eddie, walking toward the stage to sit in with Sully. Vern carried his acoustic bass guitar and Eddie held his electric 1950 Les Paul guitar. Their arrival signified that Sully was nearing the end of his set.

The crowded backstage area inspired Jesse back out to watch the rest of Sully's set. He began thinking about the mojo dust. All the pretty girls in the audience reminded him how he missed Sara. He realized he should be at home writing. Just as Jesse sensed his own restlessness, Sully's set ended.

"Sounded mighty fine there, son," Jesse said as Sully came off the stage.

"Ah, now I can ramble. Let's step back in the office." The evening's responsibility and pressure evaporated for Sully.

They entered one of the several empty rooms. The backstage crowd dispersed as the focus shifted to the Silvertones' arrival on the main stage. They performed the ritual of chopping the powder then taking turns sniffing it through a twenty-dollar bill. Jesse sensed Sully felt distracted.

"Tonight, I'm not gonna get into the zombie. I'm gonna go to a party with Annie and have some drinks."

"Okay."

"We'll hook up tomorrow."

After they sniffed several more lines of the mojo dust, they left the room. Jesse decided to go home and try to get something down on paper. Suddenly, his train of thought was broken.

"Who the fuck do you think you are?" Annie snarled, obviously drunk, approaching Jesse. Various distant crew members and security guards turned to see what all the noise was about.

"You ain't no artist! You got no friends here! Who the hell are you?" she screamed.

"I'm P.T. Barnum," he said, grinning with a sly sarcasm. Annie smiled a yellow tooth grin back at him. At least he knew that whatever flew out of her mouth was what she really thought.

Jesse walked away from them down the hallway toward the exit. His dislike of Annie had reached a severe intensity. He wondered how long he would endure this deranged woman's insults. She nurtured grave and poisonous misunderstandings concerning him. These episodes began straining his brotherhood with Sully. Everything began to sour. Jesse wondered whether this evening marked a sign of things to come.

Jesse climbed into a taxi just exited by an eager young hippie couple arriving in time for the Silvertones' show. Jesse knew Sully would stay the evening at Annie's. His mood turned black. He became tired of enduring the scorn of a confederacy of dunces. Each day revealed more reason to cut loose from the ill-informed scrutiny of such ruinous company.

Safe at home, behind locked doors, Jesse opened the bag of zombie powder. He whiffed a dangerously sized line of the rare dust. He kicked off his boots, realizing he hadn't eaten all day. He missed Sara. He began to itch from the powder as he felt a return of his creative energy. He got off the bed and sat down at the typewriter.

8

Sam hadn't slept in four days. Sunday morning came up with the dawn. He walked a short distance from a girlfriend's apartment toward the Junk House. Her kitchen clock read 6:17 a.m. when he walked out the door. He passed a twenty-four hour Dunkin' Donuts and wanted some coffee, but he had no money.

The rain cleared. Puddles of water lingered in the streets. Birds chirped. An early March sunrise made Sam Tanner yearn for the spring. He needed outdoor work. A strange desperation gripped Sam. He realized that sooner or later local drug authorities would descend upon him. Too many disturbing coincidences befell him these days. They were probably following him now for all he knew. Sam realized no wisdom existed in thumbing one's nose at the law. Soon it would be time to make a life-altering decision, quit dealing, leave town or get sober.

His drug dealing enterprises proved inefficient. It had been two weeks since the big Silvertones hometown show when he made his last real money. Sam loved mojo dust more than he loved money. As of late, he felt less regret spending his customers' money and snorting their drugs, especially people who acted disrespectful to himlike Marty Jacobs or Jethro Munroe.

He kept glancing over his shoulder expecting to see a patrol car round the corner. Lately, he remained in a constant state of nervous exhaustion. He was holding his dealer stash, but he owed money on it. His energy to sell the drugs waned, if it, ever existed in the first place.

The rising sun unsettled Sam. He felt sad, weary and broke. He let everything slip. He began to feel the damage he'd done to himself after all these years. The chirping birds haunted him in this cruel dawn. He possessed nothing to show for his folly.

Time evaporated. Pigeons eating on the sidewalk flocked away as he walked past the plant nursery. Years ago, he was a respected local carpenter, but his unpredictable and unreliable work ethic forced even his friends to stop hiring him.

He gave up everything for the sake of getting high. He sold his soul just for a thrill. He thought of his wife and daughter that he never saw anymore because of his addiction.

Sam knew he must start earning honest money. He owed many debts. He shuddered to think of all the dental work he needed. A damp breeze picked up. He walked as fast as he could. The constant fears hounded him. He felt his energy leaking away.

As Sam walked down Jupiter Avenue toward home, he thought of last night's shameful scene. Addiction served as dire motivation for his current associations. Threads of his contraband community were rotting apart and becoming increasingly risky. The sleepy charm of addiction possessed a sweet, but deadly, taste.

When Sam opened his front door, he felt happy to see the Cook, Lane and Sully sitting at the dining room table. Sam also felt happy not to see his one missing roommate, Richard Fleshman.

"Well, well, well."

"Mornin'."

"Where ya' been?"

"Over at Cynthia's," replied Sam. "Y'all hear about last night?"

"You got laid?" inquired the Cook.

"Eat shit. Last night at the Eel, Fleshman accused Jesse of being a narc. And then he punched him in the mouth."

"What?" A shocked Sully asked.

"Oh yeah. It was ugly. Jesse sliced his hand up. Fleshman was out of fucking control. He was in one of his moods."

Sam sat down at the empty chair at the wooden table. He let out a deep sigh. He removed his Chuck Taylor tennis shoes and blue ski jacket. The Cook poured the last of his dwindling stash onto the mirror as an early morning affirmation of friendship.

Sam did his line, and then produced his dealer's stash to everyone's delight. He had to sell this eight ball, but Sam went beyond the point of caring. He decided to visit his family in Mississippi next week. He'd repay the debt upon his return.

"Get out the nail," grinned Sam, determined to forget all consequences and rely on his pure savage craving.

"Hey, Hey," said the Cook, who wasn't about to argue, and disappeared to obtain his medicine bag containing instruments of vice. Sam rolled up his sleeve. Sully looked at the stash and said: "Is that an eight ball?"

Sam, acting like he didn't hear Sully's question, continued to speak about what they should be concerned about, "Fleshman was out of fucking control."

"What did Jesse do?" Sully asked.

"Well, he didn't like it. He told Fleshman he was tired of his routine. Then Fleshman sucker punched him in the mouth. Jesse smashed him in the throat and the next thing I know they're rolling around on the floor of the Eel."

"Where is Fleshman anyway?" Sully inquired. "Haven't seen him all night," replied Lane. "Jesse Wages is no fucking narc," verified Sully.

"No doubt about that," agreed Sam. "Fleshman doesn't like Jesse, so he accused him of being a narc."

"Fleshman shouldn't be accusing an innocent man. Jesse never showed up last night...and his truck was gone." Sully wondered about the location of his friend.

"Doreen wanted him to get stitches in his hand, but he just took off."

"But is there a narc?" asked Lane, pulling his chair closer to the table. The Cook returned with his black bag of needles.

"That's the question," replied Sam Tanner. "We may have an answer soon. If there is a narc, I'll bet he's sat at this very table." Sam tied a belt around his arm and began his deadly ritual with the needle and the spoon.

9

"What do you know?" Rosco Williams asked Felix in a dark corner of the Stray Cat Lounge.

"Rick Turner may have an inside line."

"Word I get, Felix Mendoza, is Tanner deals out of the Neon Eel. You can't tell me you don't know that."

"I think they're on to me."

"They better not be. You're already past the deadline I've given you."

"What do you want from me?"

"Names. I already told you goddammit!" Williams hissed. "I want names and an actual purchase that will float in court. I want to send those motherfuckers to prison. Unless you want to take their place, you should share my sense of urgency."

"Here's your last payoff." Williams handed Felix another yellow envelope.

...

Once Felix left Williams in the Stray Cat Lounge, he felt ready to carry out his evil deed. He tried to ignore and forget the haunting guilt from consequences of his past mistakes now that the money rested safely in his pocket. Felix felt like the victim of his past transgressions, yet it was too late for him to turn back now. He looked to feed off anyone he could touch.

Through savage desperation, Felix devised a new plan one that would satisfy Rosco but keep Felix from becoming the rat he never wanted to be. He knew Sam kept access to a plethora of buyers.

Felix decided to discover and expose Sam's source, hoping that a larger fish would satisfy Rosco and keep heat off Sam. Felix's only dilemma was to make sure the Junk House gang would never trace him as the narc. As a final recourse, Felix could just point the finger at Fleshman. Taking him down would be a pleasure.

Felix knew he had to raise his awareness when he was around the Junk House gang. He would look for clues amid their partying to see if he could shake loose the name or location of Sam's supplier. Felix figured he needed to be around right after Sam obtained a new stash to sell.

Suddenly, Felix remembered that Sam would be scoring today. Last Sunday morning at the Junk House, Felix overheard Sully arguing with Annie about a girl named Avalina. This beautiful young girl, Avalina, wielded a hypnotic effect on men, and the Junk House crew were no exception. The week before at The Neon Eel when the Junk House crew were all there, including Felix, Sully and Jesse, Avalina became the center of attention.

That night at The Neon Eel she innocently mentioned to Felix that Sam intended to score in a day or so. The wheels in Felix's mind turned as worlds aligned to collide.

As he thought about Sam and today's score, Felix considered Jesse Wages and Sully Sullivann were users, but they were much more distant, and more mysterious to Felix than Tanner and his gang. Felix knew Sully kept time with the Silvertones, so he remained worth watching to see where he obtained his drugs.

With thirty pieces of silver in his pocket, Felix set off for downtown to find Sam Tanner.

10

The nervewracking wait...the worst part about having an illegal vice is running out. The middleman took his money and was due to return any minute. An inherent concern about honesty regarding the deal worried him. He detested depending on someone else's honesty, rendering him vulnerable. The waiting served as exquisite torture.

A constant suspicion and lack of trust lingered concerning deals with greedy addicts in the contraband trade. It's a seller's market. An anxious grip forced a great anticipation to the limit. Drugs remained the source for such illicit friendships.

He ordered another drink. How many more dirty deals must go down before he walks away? The downtown vibration emitted evil undercurrents, month after month burning away time in a wayward fashion. A local desensitization to discretion concerning drugs remained a grave fault. A stable connection no longer existed. In such an atmosphere, stray jackals feed off someone else's generosity where no honor exists among such thieves. Everything stops for the sake of scoring because life remains boring and mundane without the drugs.

Rumor had it the local drug force had infiltrated the inner circle. One remains exposed and vulnerable for the salvation of a score and the fleeting bliss of the dust, or the last pillkeeping time in an emotional noman'sland.

Rampant impatience hounds the senses. In this era of America when no young people are being killed in war in faraway lands, he thought how his generation experienced a slower death: gradual insanity, idleness, traffic, television, voyeurism, drugs and vicarious entertainment.

For most, the American dream represents fame and fortune at any cost. Many changes lingered for the country in this antebellum year of our Lord 1995, which were unknown glory days preceding a dark era. Shattered and strange dreams exist among those who find respite in someone else's enterprises. The Internet was something people only began to hear about. AIDS sent fear in all thought processes of a generation's sexual experience, altering its mentality. No other generation experienced a threat to their natural sexual freedom. Nothing remained sacred in this new Babylon...

He looked at the clock realizing the score should already be here; he wondered about all the lost time, needless to say money and energy he expended on such vain pleasures ofthe flesh. Even if it didn't help him at the moment, he still felt it remained a pleasant waste of time. He procrastinated all regrets for later...

Jesse saw her long before anyone else in his circle of friends. She worked at Manuel's Pizza Shack as a cashier. Her nametag read AVALINA. The girl possessed an unforgettable face. Her wide, opulent, pale blue eyes; small nose and her full scarlet lips brought attention to the face with a smooth, delicate skin. Her honey colored hair went past her shoulders covering her small ears.

She was, maybe, twenty years old. Her long legs accentuated her sculptured derriere that was the shape of an upsidedown heart. She wore no bra and her small breasts and dark nipples could be clearly seen through her thin white tee shirt.

This striking girl's beauty would drive the sultan to distraction. Her smile forced one to stare. A biblical temptation lingered in her wideeyed gaze, but Jesse didn't pursue idle thoughts too long concerning such a maiden. When they first met at the pizza parlor, she said to him, "I've seen you before," as she handed Jesse his change, her long fingers touching his hand, smiling.

"Well, I stumble in and out from time to time." Jesse felt a strange disappointment on this overcast afternoon when Sully brought Avalina back to their apartment. Jesse later discovered Sully met Avalina through the Silvertones' guitar player who once dated her. Sully appeared proud to be courting a beautiful girl. He tried to avoid Annie these days.

"Avalina, this is my roommate Jesse Wages. Jesse, this is Avalina Cassidy. Y'all've met before."

"Hey, I haven't seen you since the Silvertones show," she mentioned. They shook hands and muttered greetings with somewhat embarrassed, averted glances as if they were trying to deny some unspoken connection. Jesse was impressed Sully snagged such a beauty, although, somehow, he knew their romance was likely a fleeting thing. She was certainly an upgrade from Crazy Annie. However, Jesse's instinct told him their courtship was superficial. Avalina appeared interested in Sully only for his local musical stature, and Sully only wanted her as a decoration on his arm.

Sully mixed them a bourbon and coke. He opened the kitchen drawer and pulled out the familiar powder-streaked mirror. Jesse smoked from a water pipe. He asked Ava-lina if she wanted to smoke, and she did. He showed her how to tilt the pipe to maximize the water in the chamber. Sully chopped several lines of mojo dust.

Jesse tried not to pay much attention to Avalina. He made sure his eye contact with her was minimal. Jesse felt Sully watching Avalina who watched Jesse.

Jesse sensed Sully's discomfort at the gravitation between his friend and Avalina. Jesse recalled previous conversations when Sully marvelled about how Jesse's magnetic presence appealed to women. This afternoon emerged as the first time Jesse felt Sully's marvel toward him turn to jealousy. He thought how Sully's reaction was misplaced since he knew Jesse maintained a strict code of friendship that would never allow him to pursue a friend's girl. Besides, Jesse suffered his own women problems these days.

Sully cut them each out a line. Jesse wondered what Crazy Annie was saying about Sully's new affair.

"What are you doing tonight?" Sully asked Jesse as he sniffed a line and pushed the mirror toward Avalina.

"I need to stay home and spend some time at the typewriter. Where y'all going?"

"We'll go out for a few drinks. Then I think we're having dinner at Del Rio's." Sully kissed Avalina in a rare display of public affection that seemed territorial to Jesse. She slid the empty mirror toward the middle of the table and they stood up to leave.

"You kids behave yourselves."

"Nice to see you again, Jesse," Avalina said with demure eyes then they walked out the door. Jesse sipped his drink. He reached for the telephone to call Sara. For the first time in a while, he felt alone.

12

On a dim, cold afternoon, Jethro Monroe approached Sully Sullivan in The Neon Eel. He met Sully through Jesse Wages a few weeks back. Monroe decided to seize this opportunity to converse with Sullivan when Jesse wasn't around. This continued Monroe's recent pattern of wedging his way into Jesse's circle of close friends.

Monroe believed this meeting would allow him to move past Jesse. Sully served as a direct connection to the Silvertones. All sorts of possibilities fired in Monroe's mind when he saw Sully Sullivan sitting alone at the bar.

Monroe noticed Sully talking to Doreen, who he also met through Jesse. Monroe wanted a chance to speak with Sully about managing his career, being a roadie or somehow becoming involved in the music business. Monroe thought of himself as a dealmaker.

He sat down next to the local guitar picker. Jethro pulled out his wallet attached to a chain that locked onto his belt from his back pocket as if he could influence anything by throwing around some money.

...

If Jesse knew about Monroe's ambitious intentions toward Sully, he would have never introduced them. Jesse only maintained a loose friendship with Monroe because he sold very good weed and knew other drug connections outside of the downtown loop. Jesse enjoyed having a source no one else used. He felt it gave him some privacy, control and discretion.

Lately, it became more difficult for Jesse to overlook Monroe's self-absorbed attitude. This demeanor epitomized everything Jesse felt contempt for these days. Monroe came from a wealthy family, and this financial security served as the backbone to all his logic. Monroe, a six-five, one-hundred and eighty pound, long-haired plumber, sported a beard and hair almost to his waist. His long hair and tattoos served as the costume an outlaw or renegade but could not dispel his life as a spoiled rich boy who attended an all-white private high school.

Jesse also grew tired of Monroe bragging that he obtained his drugs from same people who'd been supplying the Silvertones and Sam Tanner for years, as if he one-upped Jesse's connection to this downtown crowd.

Jesse knew Monroe's posturing betrayed a desire to play a role in the local arts scene. He coupled his outward appearance with an aggressive demeanor and countenance to frighten people. Like many know-it-alls, he possessed a zest to challenge with an insult.

Yet, as of late Jesse needed a sidekick around town. In yet another crack in his friendship with Sully, Jesse noticed Sully bonding with Fleshman. They tended to pair off when the gang was out at The Eel. They kept a lot of inside jokes.

Jesse probably liked Monroe mostly because he hated Fleshman, balancing Sully's growing love for him. Still, Jesse remembered the biblical passage stating that a man of many companions shall come to ruin.

...

"Hello Sully. Do you remember me?"

"Yeah, you're Jesse's friend, Jethro."

"Yes." They shook hands. "Where is Jesse?"

"He is with Sara. Doreen can I get another bourbon and coke?"

"Doreen, I'll pay for his drink."

"I don't pay for drinks here."

"Um, well..."

"Thanks though."

"Anytime. I'll have a Bud Lite, Doreen." Monroe dropped five dollars in the tip jar in grand fashion.

They sat in awkward silence for several minutes. Sully seemed at ease with the quiet between them, but Jethro Monroe could no longer stand the silence.

"So, does Jesse really know the actor Red Florence?"

"Oh yeah. He's introduced me to him before. Florence got Jesse on as an extra in the film Amends Unmade."

"You just can't tell about Jesse sometimes."

"Well, he's a great guy. The rascal's really my hero."

"So, ah, what do you have coming up in the future? Any gigs?"

"I'll be gone for about two weeks playing some shows out west."

After another uncomfortable silence, Jethro once again asked a question.

"Hey man, where's Sam?"

"Aw, well, actually I don't," Sully deflected. "He should be around here sometime," answered Doreen.

Sully gave her a glance as if to question whether she should be so helpful.

As Sully lit a cigarette Avalina walked in. He waited for her to approach the bar, say hello to Doreen, and then he said to Jethro: "Well, I'll see you later."

Monroe finished his beer and walked to another bar where his gang of redneck cronies kept time.

13

The March rains broke. Wet earth scents soaked the air. A tiresome chill hounded his bones. Springtime felt ages away, although the high blue sky cast a strange light as if everything were about to bloom. Fear of frosts still lingered according to local forecasts.

Jesse parked in front of Sara's townhouse. He felt lucky to arrive without incident. Many times, like this morning, he drove under the influence, or deeply fatigued from lack of sleep, both tempting fate; lately this played on his mind because usually he carried something illegal. Jesse couldn't afford any incident that would lead to a highway patrol intervention.

Sara lived in the big city, sixty miles away. He didn't show for work today. These were desperate days concerning work ethics and a creeping addiction for Jesse. He unlocked the front door. He arrived a day late. Jesse knew Sara would be angry that he failed to show up last night as they had planned.

When he entered the bedroom, he found Sara combing her hair. The TV played low. She sat on the bed wearing a tight black sweater and faded blue jeans. She wore black socks with no shoes. She began shaking her head. He knew she was angry enough to cry. Tears swelled in her dilated, hurt eyes. She never looked more beautiful to Jesse.

"How long do you think this can go on?" she asked him when their eyes met. He often asked himself the same question.

"Sara, now is not the time."

"I just took you to the hospital for getting in a fight and slicing up your hand. Things aren't getting any better. They continue to get worse."

On his drive to Sara's this morning, he experienced an anxiety attack from eating mushrooms the previous evening. Something he didn't want to deal with was staring him in the face.

"Sara, don't start in on me now."

"I can't deal with it anymore."

"Well, I can't either." He heard his voice raise.

"You're strung out. It's obvious. Look at you. You haven't slept in days. And you're driving! That's the quickest way to fuck everything up."

"I'm not gonna listen to this shit right now."

"You're going to have to make a choice."

"Sara, can I just rest right now?"

"You'll just sleep the entire weekend away. You don't include me in your plans, and yet these so-called friends of yours accuse you, of all people, of being a narc. How loyal is that?"

"That motherfucker is not my friend."

"It's beyond any one person. You're gonna regret considering these people as your friends."

Jesse looked at himself in the mirror hanging on the bedroom wall. His unwashed hair hung long and uncombed, his face needed a shave and his dilated eyes were shadowed by dark circles. He reeked of smoke, alcohol and dirty clothes since he'd not showered in several days. He knew before Sara's reprimand that he burned up his time in a wayward fashion. His damage served as the result of reckless craving and a disregard of time.

He felt them drifting apart. His lifestyle left very little time for her. He knew he should let Sara go, but his selfish needs wouldn't allow it. Writing is a hard way of life to expect a wife or girlfriend to endure. A writer in his condition was even more treacherous to a lover.

He hadn't discussed his writing with her in a long time. He knew some sort of change approached, but he couldn't tell what or when. From her deep gaze, Jesse accepted the gravity of her thoughts and concerns. An invisible anxiety began haunting him...a nagging doubt...an eerie reality.

"Sara, you're right, but you've got to let me rest. I'm sorry I didn't get over here yesterday, but I was in no shape to drive."

He could see forgiveness in her eyes, and she said, "Go sleep awhile, and later we'll go get something to eat. Give me a kiss." She hugged him.

He shed his jeans, shirt and boots then collapsed into bed. Sara turned off the television. The bright light outside made him feel guilty for not going to work. His careless youthful days faded fast. He drifted into sleep knowing he approached a personal crossroads forcing him to make a decision affecting an undetermined amount of future years. It was time to get more concerned about his craft than his friends.

14

Jethro Monroe sat in The Neon Eel displeased with his score from yesterday. By the time Monroe found Sam, the bag of mojo dust he obtained from him was a short deal. Monroe realized he did not get his money's worth. Monroe was offended that Sam employed the disrespect to treat him like an everyday street customer. He stalked into the bar searching for Sam Tanner. He prepared to wait the next several hours out to confront Sam.

"Hello, Doreen."

"Hey, Jethro. You looking for Jesse?"

"No, actually I'm looking for Sam."

"I haven't seen him today. What do you want to drink?"

"I'll have a Bud Lite. Speaking of the devil, have you seen Jesse?"

"He and Sully hung out for awhile last night."

"Hey, Doreen, hold off on that beer. I'm gonna go check a couple more bars for Tanner and I'll be back later."

"Sure."

Doreen felt glad to see him go.

. . .

On a Tuesday afternoon on the thirty-first day of March, while birds chirped at sunset, Jesse knocked on the Junk House front door. He stared at the row of boxwoods and crepe myrtle trees alongside the house before a grinning Sam Tanner answered the door by saying: "When things go well, they go really well."

Sam gestured for Jesse to enter. He sat in the living room. Sam's long awaited score finally rested on the table. Early evening sunlight faded through the cheap, yellow curtains. Sam stood to make a big profit if he acted prudently in his transactions. He usually snorted into what he intended to sell so he had to short someone along the way, most likely one of his least favorite customers, to break even on a deal. He'd stay high for weeks if things developed as planned.

"Ah, there is nothing like the security of having a big stash of pure cocaine," mentioned Sam, staring as he cut corners out of plastic sandwich bags, weighed the dust on a scale and prepared the bindles for distribution.

"I haven't really got to talk to you much since you got back from Mississippi. How was all that?" asked Jesse.

"It's always good for me to go there. I see my Dad. I dry out. I usually come back with a little money."

"Last time I saw you..."

"Yeah, times were ugly. I straightened out a couple things with certain people since I've been back. It's business as usual. I just needed to get out of town for a while."

After Sam divided and weighed the mojo dust on an electronic scale, he took a large sniff of the bitter powder and rubbed a bit on his gums as well to numb the pain of his rotting incisor and cuspid teeth.

He used a butter knife to cut the brick. It looked like new pool chalk. Sam distributed the small crystals, powder and larger rocks into the small plastic bags. An intense and strange scent rose up from the newspaper where Sam kept the dust.

"It looks like golf balls," said Jesse in amazement as he watched Sam hold the bag up to the light like a prize.

"Yes, indeed. That smell. It's pure, uncut shit. Listen, I've got a couple of friends coming over in a few minutes. I'll get you a little package together. First, cut us out a couple nice lines."

With his Swiss army knife, Jesse shaved a chunk from the mother lode. He had never seen this much pure mojo dust before. It produced a smell that made his stomach turn.

An open window blew a soft, mild breeze through the dusty living room. The sky reddened in the west. A chill circulated throughout the house. Sam returned from the kitchen and began cutting corners from more baggies.

Jesse handed an empty pen shaft used for snorting powder to Sam, who deferred by saying:

"Go ahead."

"Thanks."

Jesse snorted two of the four lines. He almost gagged as he swallowed the bitter crystals. His head cleared.

He tasted the bitter powder in the back of his throat. His forehead went numb. He sweated a little. Sam dropped three nickelsized rocksover three grams into a bag, tied the corners and handed it to Jesse with a grin.

"Here you go, my man."

"Damn Sam, that's a healthy dose."

"This one is on the house...enjoy it, my brother."

"Thanks."

"Come back later and we'll have some drinks we might get a game of poker going."

"Well, I never know when Fleshman is gonna be here."

"Don't worry about Fleshman."

"I still can't get over that bullshit, but fuck it."

"That's the spirit, now listen...is this guy Jethro, is he a friend of yours? Because I don't like that guy."

"Hey, I don't blame you. Don't do anything you don't feel good about. I don't know about anyone other than myself these days."

"Well, fair warning."

"Duly noted. Thank ye' kindly...I'll see you later."

Jesse realized how healthy the stash Sam kind-heartedly gave him was when he felt it in his pocket as he walked across the street. Jesse looked forward to enjoying such a stash safe at home alone.

Using the dust tonight would be a good time to type up a bunch of pages. He hardly ever began a story while high on mojo dust; if he started while sober and almost finished, he might be able to end the story, but other than that he found the drug useless, unless sleeplessness, nervousness, and craving was his intention.

His stated design for this drug remained the creative productivity. This was what he always told himself was the kick about getting high anyway. He wanted to channel the energy. He remembered when he first started smoking how it seemed to open and uninhibit his mind when he wrote. Tonight was a rare occasion when he sat alone with only his typewriter and a strong stash of high-grade dust.

Jesse realized how fortunate he was to leave work early, enabling him to obtain the dust from Sam this afternoon. The people at work liked him, but Jesse felt like they watched him out of the corner of their eyes. He knew his appearance made it clear to most he didn't want to move into management. Jesse wondered whether his co-workers suspected his clandestine rituals.

He knew this job wasn't his lifelong livelihood. Most of whom arrived fresh out of college and entering management remained the only way to earn real money with the corporation. After three years with the company, he had arranged part time work hours without feeling any resistance from upper-management.

He needed a job that allowed him to prioritize his writing but still helped him pay for day-to-day essentials. He only worked the job a few hours each day, but the work thoroughly bored him. As of late, Jesse felt like even the small amount of effort the agency required of him squandered his creative energy.

Jesse wondered what these crystals he dumped out onto the house mirror had to do with his future. He crushed the rocks into dust with a tablespoon. He put on *Kind of Blue* and cut out two lines of dust with a stray joker card from his new deck. He sniffed the lines one after the other, alternating nostrils. The ritual of chopping the powder had become as addictive as snorting it.

Soon, the white line fever gripped him. He hoped no unexpected visitors would stop by the apartment; he wanted no distractions or disturbances, but anxiety always lingered because he could never be sure who might show up, or when these days.

Jesse gathered the pages he needed to retype. He intended to complete this short story he'd been writing for a week. He looked out the window and decided he wanted to get as much done as possible. Staring at the John Coltrane poster hanging on the wall, he forgot about late rent, how he missed Sara and how he remained overwhelmed by his consistent state of poverty.

He resumed his writing ritual at the typewriter. After another line, and another thirty minutes, he reread what he'd typed up. He heard the neighbor's dog across the street barking. The neighbors downstairs were cooking their usual currysmelling dish.

Darkness fell. Jesse looked out the kitchen window and stood up. The dust made him pace the floors. He was only about halfway finished revising the short story. Jesse again heard the neighbor's dog barking. Things began to take on a surreal vibration when he snorted another two lines. The atmosphere of the apartment began to disturb him.

He felt an electric current in the air he could not comprehend. It almost seemed someone lurked in the room with him, but no one was there. Besides the dog barking, things were too quiet. He and Sully had been listening to a lot of talk and sports radio lately, but tonight Jesse kept the radio turned off, opting for Miles Davis instead. He hadn't been sleeping well, and a head laced full of good mojo dust wouldn't help him rest. His stash sitting out in the open on the kitchen table made him increasingly nervous.

Jesse heard the neighbor's dog bark before, but now he was sure it was barking at something specific. He thought about how he'd not eaten all day, but now it was too late. He returned to his typewriter trying to progress the story.

Jesse read what he'd written and then resumed pacing the floor, hoping this would help him decide how to end the story. He felt on the edge of something. He returned to the ritual with the mirror.

As he paced toward the window, he suddenly noticed the flashing lights of three police cars outside the Junk House. Jesse's blood froze as a nauseating wave burned through his stomach. He wondered if his mind was playing tricks on him for a moment before realizing this must be why the dog was barking.

His mind raced. He began pacing. He didn't want to look out the window too many times, but he could only wonder what the cops were doing there, and whatever reason it was, it couldn't be good.

He knew Sam expected company, and he wondered if the rumors of the local task force had become a reality. He immediately hid his stash out of sight in the bathroom. He could only think of two reasons why the cops would be there, and with no ambulances around, only one.

For the next twenty minutes, Jesse could not concentrate on anything. He remained distracted, pacing the floors and peering out the window at any sound. Had they planned to bust Sam? Jesse wondered if this strange evening could be an ominous sign at hand.

He pondered the trouble a man can get into for the flowers of indulgence. All sorts of scenarios passed through his mind. A severe price taxes the soul for following a wayward procession of ancient temptation.

The cop cars remained parked outside the Junk House while Jesse forced himself to read his story from beginning to end. He wanted to read it aloud, but he couldn't bring himself to betray the silence. The mojo dust raced within him creating a serious distraction, and the police scenario rendered him beyond nervous.

He remembered countless evenings when he got high all night on only a fraction of what he snorted this evening. Jesse opened the refrigerator and stared at the empty shelves. There were some old tangerines and weekold Chinese food on the shelves, but no beer.

Once again he peered out the kitchen window. The cop cars remained. A few minutes later, he heard a knock at the door. His stomach tightened, and his blood ran cold. He prepared to see cops as he looked through the peephole.

Instead, he opened the door, and Sam Tanner stood there looking as if he had been embalmed. Sam's skin appeared a cadaverous shade of pale.

"C'mon in, Sam." Jesse closed the door and locked it.

"Well, you missed it."

"What the fuck was that all about? I saw the cop cars parked outside."

"Lennear and I were in the back, mainlining the shit, when we heard someone banging on the fucking door."

"Why?"

"Turns out Lennear made a call on the phone I brought back from my mother's house, and because my Dad is in such bad shape, she had 911 programmed, and Lennear accidentally hit the button."

"Did they come in?"

"They asked if there was a problem. 'No problem here I say." Sam stood in the kitchen sweating profusely. He kept licking his untrimmed moustache. A look of fear glowed in Sam's eyes that Jesse had never seen before.

"Have a seat," Jesse said. "I wish I had a beer to offer you. Man, I saw those cop cars, and I knew there was trouble."

"When I heard someone pounding on the door, I thought somebody was fucking around. It was me, Doreen, and Lennear...hell, I thought it might be you. I opened the door holding my arm and there stood three police officers. Luckily I had on a long sleeve shirt to cover my arm.

"I almost had a fucking heart attack. Lennear is holding a half an ounce and so am I the cops step in, there's residue everywhere, and if they'd looked close enough, we'd have been fucked. I explained about the phone. I apologized and somehow convinced them everything's okay, and they left...miraculously. But they were suspicious and lingered for a while asking questions."

Sam wiped the sweat from his forehead and said, "Anyway, Doreen invited us back to the Eel for a drink. You want to come along?"

"I need to stay here and work since I'm in the zone. Stop by on the way back if you want though.

"Well, you got lucky and missed that excitement."

"Saved me more damage to my nervous system."

"I'll see you after a while."

"Have fun," Jesse said, and they laughed, but Sam remained visibly rattled. Jesse patted him on the back as he walked out the door.

Tonight's episode unsettled Jesse. They all escaped unscathed, so surely this incident served as some distant warning. Jesse's mind became overwhelmed with eerie questions. Would the authorities ignore such a situation? Would the Junk House go under local surveillance now? Surely this blunder would not go unnoticed by the authorities. Jesse tried to remain detached and unseen, but he lived too close to these people to be excluded from police scrutiny.

Jesse sat amazed at how much of the stash Sam gave him he'd already consumed. This didn't stop Jesse from fiendishly snorting more dust into the early hours of the next morning. He tried to keep working because he knew he couldn't fall asleep, but he was exhausted. He began to loathe this room and these daily circumstances.

Jesse crawled into bed at 7:47 a.m. Sam never returned, and Jesse hadn't seen Sully in days. Jesse tried deep breathing to calm down, but his racing mind couldn't shake this mercurial line of truth and illusion that began blurring.

It would be another day before Jesse actually fell asleep. He regretted not spending time with Sara, feeling like a castaway soul.

15

Felix ordered a vodka and cranberry from Doreen just as The Neon Eel opened for the day. Doreen kept busy in her diurnal bar duties of as slicing cocktail fruit, unlocking pool tables and preparing the bar for another business evening.

It was a warm Wednesday afternoon. Felix stared at a local newspaper trying to appear casual. Doreen's usual musical rotation of the Grateful Dead played over the cantina speakers.

"Doreen, what do you say me and you elope together?"

"Felix, don't be coming in here with your twisted notions of romance."

Felix was desperate for a friend. He chuckled to himself. They did not speak for a few minutes while Doreen waited on several regulars. Felix lit a Marlboro and watched a motorcycle race on the television mounted above the bar. Doreen was slicing lemons when Felix whispered: "Doreen, who has the best connection in this town?"

"Y'know, Felix, that's a strange question considering we've only spoken about this to each other maybe two times, but I'm not sure."

"Aw, c'mon, Doreen, you can trust me." She looked up at him, then returned to slicing lemons, and replied: "It's not that I don't trust you, but you're in the know just as much as I am."

"I've been hearing some interesting rumors about Sam's source. You know anything about that?"

"No, I don't", Doreen moved away from Felix to avoid further questioning. She remained at the far end of the bar talking to several regulars.

Felix turned pages of the local newspaper without reading anything. "Doreen, just one more please," Felix said in a resigned fashion, sliding an empty glass across the bar.

She made the drink without a word. The bar became more crowded.

"Do you know where Sam scores from?" he asked Doreen in a hushed tone when she gave him his drink.

"I sure don't, Felix, but I know he has several sources." She quickly walked away toward the opposite end of the bar to discourage his line of questioning.

Felix gulped down his strong drink and left The Neon Eel. He walked to Manuel's. Felix called Rosco Williams's answering machine and punched in a code to hear a message recorded specifically for him. He listened to his latest instructions: "Hog's Breath, you got lucky. Something's taken precedent over your situation for several weeks. Find real work until then and check this message three weeks from today."

Felix hung up the phone and considered his options. He could leave town now would be a good time but what he really wanted was a friend to confide in to share the burden of his sinister secret.

...

A fever dream conjures some distant ghost parade. Castaway souls remain scattered like windswept brown leaves along a lost highway. Blooming seasons remembered in tainted tomorrows amid soiled yesterdays...tortured pilgrims arrive in obscure congregations...washed-out eyes under a bone-colored sun straining to see the eternal hourglass elapsing forever. A strange coincidence fills these days. Barstool blues craving salvation while veiling a false friendship for hidden motivations marring all goodwill. A trail of vultures wait at the red river of wine...

Today's friend is tomorrow's enemy. Self-imposed tests revealed codes of weak temperance in such drug, trade adventures. Crafty companions and cravings prevail amid selfish motives and evil barters cast liens on the soul. False friends lure with late-night promises. Signs of decay and dissipation remained everywhere. His motivation revolved around quenching the thirst of addiction.

He awoke in a cold sweat biting his hand.

16

Tonight Nancy Mulberry hosted a grand birthday party for an employee at her other upscale restaurant, Shiro's. The establishment was decorated for this festive gathering, which included an open bar and sushi buffet for invited guests only.

The Junk House gang sat in the back of the bar away from the party. Only Fleshman was late. Sam, the Cook and Lane Lennear waited on him; it would be the first time in weeks all the roommates sat in one place at the same time. They intended to discuss household bills and debts amid Nancy's hospitality. Nancy understood the psychic weather of these fellows and decided to let them meet here away from their home turf.

This was not their type of crowd, but Nancy always kept a soft spot for this crew so she allowed them to stay in a back corner where they could drink and eat for free, as long as they didn't cause trouble. While waiting, they took it upon themselves to partake in all of the free Sapporo beer and sushi they could consume.

"Why is it the only time Fleshman is not around is when we're about to discuss money?" asked Sam as he drank warm sake, wiping wasabi on his dirty jeans while watching the festive party fill up the restaurant. Patrons were dressed in casual evening clothes while this gang wore ripped jeans and tee shirts.

"He owes eight hundred dollars and we all know it," remarked Lennear. Just as Lennear made the statement Fleshman walked through Shiro's front door. He carried a brown grocery bag while wearing a black tee shirt, cut off army pants, railroad cap, ponytail and black, hightop Chuck Taylors. After briefly talking with several people, he made his way back to their table.

"Y-y-you're never on time," stuttered the Cook, gazing up from his tome on voodoo.

"Better late than never," retorted Fleshman.

"This month's rent is due, and you still haven't paid for December, January, February, or March yet," Lennear said to Fleshman.

"You'll get your fucking money, Lane, you stingy fucker."

"Everybody has to pull their weight," said Sam to Fleshman.

"What I need to do is get my own fucking place," said Fleshman with an air of threatening contempt.

"Oooh yeah, you'll be able to afford that," said the Cook, this time not looking up from his book.

"At least there will be peace and quiet. I won't have to worry about the cops busting in."

"You need to pay what you owe first then get your own place if that's what you want," Lane Lennear said with a cold finality.

"Don't worry," sneered Fleshman, "when I finish this job, I'll be caught up."

"Just pay the money," muttered Sam.

"Get fucking Felix to pay. He's there more than I am. Who the fuck is he anyway, Sam? You're the one he follows around like a puppy dog."

"Some dude I met at the bar last year."

"Make him pay some fucking rent. Here's two hundred dollars." Fleshman handed the money to Lennear. "That's all I have till I get this job finished."

"F-F-Felix makes me nnnervous, too," said the Cook.

"He's been acting weird lately, weirder than usual," reiterated Fleshman, "asking where Cook scores, and then he disappears when we do. Have I told you Nancy thinks he's a narc?" Fleshman asked Sam.

"Everyone is an informant to you. You see betrayal everywhere. By the way, don't accuse Jesse of being a narc anymore. He's as much a narc as you."

"Hey, I made a mistake. Don't bring that up again. Listen to this, Nancy swears she saw Felix drinking in the Stray Cat Lounge with this fucking narcotics agent Rosco Williams. She went to high school with Williams, and she's sure it was him."

"Felix is a blunt New Yorker; he'll talk to anyone about anything," explained Sam. "So what if he's a cop?" Sam then released a powerful effluvium.

"Fool yourself if you want, but you know what Nancy says makes sense," said Fleshman. "He always leaves right after we score like he has to go make a call or something." Fleshman appeared annoyed, and continued speaking to Sam in a more severe tone.

"Didn't I hear him say he got busted a while back? Remember last year when he was dealing. Then he quit dealing, disappears for a couple months, now he's back strong as ever. It stinks to me. I don't want that fucker around my house anymore. Sam, you're too fucking reckless down at the Eel. You can't go throwing somebody's stash up on the bar just to thumb your nose at the law."

"You sound paranoid."

"Paranoia is an irrational fear. There's nothing irrational being concerned about getting thrown in prison for dealing drugs. That's a strong possibility for you at this point, and I want no part of that."

"Thanks for your concern," Sam deadpanned. "Now, you should speak to your accountant concerning your residential debts."

"Whatever."

Sam stayed at Shiro's while his roommates went home or moved on to another bar. As much as Sam rejected Fleshman's assertions, he knew he'd become careless. Through convenience and laziness, Sam did most of his dealing in The Neon Eel to the point that everyone knew they could find him there at certain hours in the afternoon.

Even worse, he'd begun selling drugs to anyone and everyone. Sam attracted these strangers, and deep down he enjoyed the attention of people always looking for him. However, he realized that his flagrant disregard for contraband discretion and etiquette would sooner or later catch up to him. He also understood the dangerous game he played by cheating customers with diluted product to make up for all the drugs he and his friends consumed without compensation.

Unfortunately, his appetite for the dust remained stronger than his love for money. With the help of the Cook, Sam had access to high-grade drugs. Next week they intended to score a quarter ounce of zombie powder on top of last week's mojo dust. A constant downtown demand existed for all brands of contraband powder. An increasing number of people Sam didn't even know approached him for drugs, and he almost always obliged them.

Sam realized the unfriendly locals saw him as a drug dealer and lowrent con artist. He knew downtown loyalties swayed with the wind. Sam became tired of his dirty dealings, but his options remained limited.

He smoked another cigarette. If intoxication remained his salvation, he was long ago baptized in this river of fire. Yet, Sam, a fisher of lost men, occasionally cheated his customer with friendly aplomb, smoothing over the deal with his lighthearted countenance and good-natured, apologetic excuses making it difficult for most to remain angry.

The Local Stranger

He looked forward to Monday when he and the Cook would score. He needed to lower his profile since he was aware the way word traveled as of late, but he stood to make a lot of money. He made a promise to himself to fade from the dealing scene after this round. He wanted to be only an anonymous user and not a dealer.

Sam drank another bottle of sake and left the party. He went to see a lady friend intending to spend the evening with her.

17

On a late April afternoon Jesse walked downtown. He could not force himself to sit at the typewriter, so he decided to prowl the bars. Knowing he'd encounter the same ruinous patrons when he frequented his several favorite bars reminded him he should be at home working. He finally arrived under the canopy at the Jamaican Grill where he drank a beer and began to write a story with no end in a pocket notebook. At least today was payday.

"Hey, Jesse." He looked up and noticed Avalina standing over him. She wore cutoff blue jeans and an Atlanta Braves baseball shirt. She pulled a chair up next to him. He closed his notebook.

"Hey, Avalina, what's happening?"

"I quit my job today."

"At the camera shop?"

"I could never make it on time."

"Oh well. Que Sera, Sera."

"I've quit three jobs in a month."

"It ain't easy getting up these days, is it?"

"Or going to sleep. I appreciate you not minding that I stay over at y'all's place since I lost my apartment."

"It's no problem."

"Can I return the favor?"

"You have some?"

"Yes, let's walk across the street." They drifted inside the Dream Time Bar. The place remained quiet in the afternoon. They ducked into the women's bathroom and Avalina locked the stall. Jesse admired the way she took charge. They stood very close together.

Avalina looked radiant. Her golden hair fell down below her shoulders. She had huge, pale blue eyes. A distant scent of chamomile emanated from her skin in the humid air. Avalina kept her stash in a secret pocket in the front of her black underwear. She shut the stall and he couldn't tell what she was doing down there. For a moment he thought she was hiding the stash in her pussy, and it turned him on.

"My secret pocket. I figure they'll never search me there." Jesse was tempted to smell the bag when she handed it to him. He opened the small bag. They used Jesse's house key as a spoon.

When they sniffed the powder their faces remained close together. Jesse felt a strong sexual undercurrent between them, and although they both realized the attraction, he refused to act upon the raw emotion despite its power. Ever since he first met her, he fought the temptation to kiss her full lips, because Jesse knew she was a very impressionable girl.

Jesse's aloofness only served to attract Avalina. They'd been having more and more one-on-one conversation. Over the past couple of weeks as Avalina had taken up temporary residence in the apartment. Jesse was a good conversationalist, which further attracted her to him. He always enjoyed the way she looked at him.

They finished several turns and walked undetected out of the ladies room and back across the street. Avalina ordered a beer and sat down next to Jesse. A sudden breeze blew from the north. Few cars traveled this part of town during afternoon hours so traffic remained light. An elderly woman walked her dog. A young couple looked in the window of a nearby furniture store.

Avalina lit a cigarette. Jesse felt as if he was on the pulse of everything. This was a significant change from how he felt when he walked into The Jamaican Grill.

"Sully's coming back Friday, because he's got a show Saturday, right?" Jesse asked.

"I think so. It seems he's been gone longer than two weeks. Annie keeps trying to sabotage us. She hates me, and I hate her. It'll come to a head when he gets back.

I can't stand her."

"She gets on everyone's nerves."

"She's trying to pit me and Sully against each other."

"Yeah, me, too."

Avalina watched him with a receptive smile.

"You know, that barroom episode still bothers me. Sully told me he felt sorry about it. Still, Fleshman told me in a room full of people that he was gonna fuck my brains out. I think that deserves some response, right?"

"Classy guy...he's just another idiotic asshole to me. I couldn't fathom saying that to my friend's girlfriend."

"I'm sorry I brought him up."

"He'll come up again, don't worry."

"So, you and Sara still aren't speaking?"

"Not really. We don't really get along these days. It's a come and go blues."

A familiar schoolboy friend of Avalina's walked up and said hello to her. Many fellows sought her attention, but she remained sitting next to Jesse. He continued to mute any sexual waves toward her because of Sully.

He was sexually attracted to her, but he talked to her as if she were his sister. He never wanted to give the impression he was coming on to her, if anything, he made sure he acted disinterested. Even though his friend created this tempting situation, Jesse could not bring himself to betray Sully and sleep with Avalina. There was Sara to think of, too.

Jesse knew many guys blatantly were trying to tempt her into the bedroom with drugs these days. Her increasing taste for powders began to attract many of these nightcrawlers.

Jesse playfully scratched Avalina's head as he stood up to leave and told her he'd see her later. He walked home intending to work and prepare for the change that approached. He pondered how it would all boil down to the present moment.

...

Later that night, while Jesse catnapped on the couch, Avalina stumbled into the apartment. The candle burning on the kitchen table was the only light shining in the apartment. He opened his eyes and saw her standing above him.

"Avalina?"

"Did I wake you?"

"I was having a bizarre dream."

"Tell me," Avalina said as Jesse rubbed his eyes. "Where have you been tonight?" he asked. "Downtown drinking."

"You're a bad girl," muttered Jesse as he glanced at her chest. She sat on the couch beside him and lit a cigarette. Silver flashes lit up her eyes again enticing Jesse to kiss Avalina's lush lips.

"What were you dreaming about?" she asked, leaning her face closer to his.

"Uh, well...I'm not sure I want to say..."

"Aw, c'mon. Tell me. I'm a big girl."

"Well, to tell the truth, I dreamed I was teaching an old girlfriend to eat pussy." Avalina's eyes dilated and she began breathing through her mouth, "Hmmmm..."

"Have you ever thought about it?" Jesse asked this revealing question as if he were still asleep.

"Eating another girl's pussy? No, not really. But I guess if it were the right girl...you ever think about another guy?"

"Never."

"I didn't think so."

Avalina's eyes were now catlike. He felt her watching him, smiling through her cigarette smoke. Jesse felt the pendulum of sexual attraction swinging dangerously close. After a few moments of frustrating silence from Jesse, Avalina said, "I gotta leave this town."

Her blue eyes became reflective and melancholy. Jesse watched her exhale smoke and then put out the cigarette in an empty beer bottle on the coffee table. Images of Avalina passed through his mind he could not talk about. He thought of Sara and said, "Me, too."

"I think Sully and I are finished."

"Why do you say that? This sure is a change from our conversation earlier today. Besides, he's not even back yet."

"I can feel it. It's just not working."

"I understand the sentiment. This is not a real good atmosphere for lovers."

"Crazy Annie has ruined everything. I'm sick of her."

"Let's don't get started on that conversation."

"I'm sorry. You're right." Another pregnant silence arose between them. Jesse rubbed his eyes. He knew that without Sara or Sully in the picture, he'd kiss this girl passionately, hoping to make the most intimate contact with her.

"Jesse," she whispered, peering into his eyes, "what do you think of me?"

"I love you to death...you're like my little sister."

"I think you're the cat's meow," she said as they both laughed.

"You know I feel the same way about you."

"I'm not sure I can come on any stronger."

"If Sully wasn't a friend, Avalina, and Sara wasn't my girlfriend, I'd want you all for myself."

"Sully isn't an issue for me. So he shouldn't be for you."

"It isn't that simple between friends, Avalina. Do you have any dust left?"

"I'm all out. I felt it was my turn to take care of my friends. By the time I shared with everyone, there was none left... I really need to quit."

"Well, we all should take a break from time to time." Jesse searched for words as the temptation to kiss Avalina overwhelmed him. To further tamp down his passions, he thought of the scandalous row that would ensue if he kissed her. Of course, the story would be that Jesse moved in on his best friend's girl rather than the truth that Avalina was tired of the relationship with Sully. Jesse knew this would give the downtown jackals further reasons to play him as the scapegoat.

Between his fatigue and the temptations that Avalina offered, Jesse's mind raced through conversations he and Sully had about Avalina. He remembered Sully saying Avalina was too young to perform proper fellatio, but since he only bathed once every two or three weeks that may have discouraged her. What a derogatory statement to make about this young beauty willing to share an intimate moment.

Jesse thought about how Sully's lethal jests would catch up with him one day; out of the spite in that moment, Jesse wanted to have her for himself. To Sully everything was a joke. A shot of sarcasm truth with a cheap laugh chaser. He didn't deserve her.

"I'm leaving this town," Avalina said, interrupting Jesse from his thoughts. "Two weeks ago my Mom had to come get me."

"From here?"

"I couldn't take it."

"What did she say?"

"She freaked out and cried. My Dad did his best to be cool. They're both freaked out over my situation."

"Like I said, we all need a break."

"Remember when we used to see each other when I worked at Manuel's?"

"That was before we knew who the other was."

"We sort of fell for each another, didn't we?"

"Until we realized we're victims of circumstance."

"But you're still one of my favorite people." She touched his face then asked, "Knowing what is going on with you two, do you think Sara would care?"

"She wouldn't like it. Neither would Sully."

"Then, we can be quiet about it. No one would know. It's just me and you." He could feel her voice becoming deeper, almost a purring whisper.

This moment bordered on the surreal.

"Let's wait until, y'all officially break up." Avalina sighed with exasperation and said, "It's funny, the ones you want never really go for you."

"That's not it at all."

"Then kiss me."

"If I do I'll never stop."

"I wouldn't let you stop."

"Avalina, you're not making this easy on me."

"Good! I don't want to. Can't you see the way I look at you? I want to smell your skin when I'm next to you." She leaned over and kissed him. Jesse acted passive, but he did not resist. She slipped her tongue into his mouth. They kissed momentarily and then Avalina stood up when it was clear he wasn't going to respond in kind.

"I won't put you through this. I have to go," she said.

"Avalina, listen..."

"Don't say anything, Jesse. At least you know how I feel about you now." She slipped into her sweater and was out the door. Gone. Jesse's head reeled. Alone in the apartment again, it seemed spirits haunted him at all hours.

18

The next day, a brief calm soothed his mind now that his pay-check rested in his pocket. The money would not last, but he'd be able to obtain a long-awaited score. Some time elapsed since any zombie powder appeared on the local scene. He hoped to avoid the addict's irony that when one had money, there was no stash to be found, and vice versa.

Jesse sneezed while he wandered downtown. He sought out Sam. He remained the only person Jesse trusted to obtain this rare contraband. Jesse had only seen Sam a few times since he returned from his father's funeral a couple weeks ago. Jesse told himself this would be his last score for a while. He became all too aware how drugs transform people's personalities and lives; everything sold for sake of dust.

He missed Sara.

He couldn't find Sam in either of his usual haunts. Jesse refused to speak with anyone else, so he walked home without having a drink. As he walked he noticed the sky looked different. Constant change never ceases. A touch of mystery lingered in the sky.

His attention span returned to vice. A stone cold fever awakened a sinister reality. Jesse stopped by the Junk House on his way home, expecting Sam not to be there. Jesse stood surprised when Sam answered his knock at the door.

"Hey, ol' boy."

"Jesse, c'mon in." They embraced. Jesse was surprised to see Sam alone in the house.

"How ya' doing, Sam?"

"I'm about to get the fuck out of here." Sam acted like he didn't want to talk about his recent loss, and Jesse never forced him. The Junk House stood eerily quiet. Sam appeared nervous.

"You wouldn't by chance have anything, would you?"

"Today is your lucky day. I've got a half gram of some wicked zombie powder."

"How much?"

"I'll give it to you for seventy five dollars if you give me a line."

"It's a deal."

"This is all I have left," said Sam, "so make it last."

He retrieved the small bag from a cigar box by the mirror. The sparse room was in disarray. His bed was a stack of crates covered with a mattress. A busted television sat on a bureau and a pile of sour old clothes sat abandoned in the middle of the room. Sam had gained even more weight over the past few months. His breathing was heavy, and he constantly sweated.

"You okay?" Jesse asked, giving him a playing nudge in the arm as Sam cleared a place on the small table to put the drugs.

"Well, I owe money, and they're looking for me." Sam handed the small bag to Jesse. Jesse dipped into it with his Swiss army knife and laid Sam a little dust on the cigar box. The score looked a little slack, but Jesse did not mention it.

"I'm gonna leave you in peace now. Thanks, Sam."

"Be careful."

"You, too."

Jesse went home and locked the door. He felt a morbid sadness about his excitement over having a full stash of smack. He hoped Sully would stop by so he could share his rare contraband. Somehow he thought that would make him feel better about it.

The first small line he indulged in washed over him like a sonic wave. He felt nauseated and his ears began to flutter. Soon, his face began itching. He began the ritual again for the other nostril. Then he put it away.

All people, places and concerns faded. A new optimism appeared. After a few minutes waiting for the medicine to take its full effect, he went into the bathroom and threw up. The dull mid-day sun shined through the windows giving Jesse now a mindset of foreboding.

Disconnected with time, he almost felt clairvoyant or telepathic. He knew change was at hand. He closed his eyes. A symphony of demons danced in his mind. They taunted and laughed at him. Sheets of maroon flame burned his imagination. He sat back at the kitchen table staring at the typewriter.

He thought again of Sara.

Two hours later, he resumed the ritual two more times. This batch seemed a little gritty to him. He looked at his strange reflection in the mirror. His pupils were pinpoints and his skin took on a cadaverous shade of pale when he went back to the bathroom. It seemed something was very wrong. A powerful guilt descended on him.

He felt depressed. He pulled his work pages out, but he didn't have the focus to reread anything. He stumbled into the bathroom and got sick again. He sat back down in front of the typewriter.

An hour or so later, a startling knock at the front door roused Jesse. Before he could get up, Doreen stuck her head inside.

"Anybody home?"

"Come on in, Doreen."

"Hey boy. Damn, you feel okay?"

"I'm a little out of it."

"You look green."

"I feel weird. I just got sick. I got some of that stuff from Sam."

"C'mon boy get up. We're going for a ride. You need some fresh air."

Jesse stood up, walked down the steps and got in Doreen's Chevy truck.

"When did you see Sam?"

"A couple of hours ago."

"I hope he starts using his head. His source got busted this morning."

"Really? Sam didn't mention it."

"They raided his house and caught him with-listen to this-84 grams of coke, ten bags of zombie powder..."

"Oh no..."

"One pound of reefer, one bag of mushrooms and some crystal meth. They raided his house at about 6 a.m. Someone ratted him out. The shit has hit the fan."

"Doreen, pull over."

He threw up green bile on the dirt road right off Sycamore Avenue.

"I've got something to wake you up. It's at the house. It's been a strange day."

...

He bought a piece of Doreen's mojo dust stash from her, and they stayed up talking all night. On her way to work at noon, she dropped him off at home. He snorted his last two lines at the kitchen table where the evening began last night. He was exhausted. He felt like he was at a scene of a crime. He was in unholy shambles.

Recent events had him considering leaving town. He thought more of Sara and a quieter place to work. All sensible roads led back to money and employment. He had reached a dead end here.

There were countless distractions to his writing. Jesse felt the wear and tear on the relationships with some of his friends due to daily exposure. At the same time, seeking independence from them made him feel isolated. He no longer thrived on it like he did a few years ago. Jesse realized he needed to be with Sara. He had to see if they could survive as a couple, and if his writing could flourish in another environment.

He walked downtown to visit the three music stores, and two bookstores and get something to eat. He wished he could buy all sorts of music and books, but he had no money to make a purchase. In the face of life-altering decisions, he couldn't lose himself in the music or stories.

He felt some obscure inertia pressing against him as if a sad farewell were at hand. He remembered several eras in his life, but nothing eluded him like the present moment.

He strolled into the downtown pawnshop trying again to lose himself amid books, old albums, lamps, antiques, instruments, clothing, furniture, tools, silverware, trinkets and whatever esoterica he scanned as he tried to unlock the solution to his dilemma.

After several hours, Jesse decided to visit The Burrito Bar and enjoy his usual black bean and rice deluxe burrito with no tomatoes, chips and a water chaser. On the way home he felt nauseated. He understood his path ahead would be painful.

19

"Mendoza, this is your last dance," uttered Rosco Williams, squinting through cigarette smoke. The two men sat across from each other in their same cantina.

"I've never been able to find out a direct source. Hell, I figured they scored from the guy who just got busted.

"Tanner deals out of The Neon Eel and you know it. He's taking a dive, so will you if you don't get something we can use in court. We've got evidence to issue a warrant for the arrest of Sam Tanner.

"I think they're onto me," Felix Mendoza said in a voice as if he might be spared such a reality.

"You're being paranoid, Mendoza."

"What do you expect after this recent bust? So, what do you want me to do again?"

"You must be on the scene when the bust goes down. We need you there to make a purchase. That's the only way you get off."

"I'm fucked."

20

Jesse entered The Neon Eel when the bar opened. He saw Sam Tanner sitting at the table in front of the TV. Jesse's spirit lifted. He felt relieved to see Sam after the news of the bust that Doreen shared with him last week.

After noticing Doreen wasn't behind the bar, Jesse bought a beer and sat down next to Sam under a dim light at the shotout gambling table, a cheap novelty of the bar. A pack of Marlboros, today's newspaper, one sheet of paper and a green Bic lighter sat in front of Sam on the worn felt gambling table. Jesse sensed trouble.

"I heard there was a bust, Sam. What's shaking?"

"Well, a friend of mine made me a copy of this," and he handed Jesse a xeroxed page. The piece of paper revealed that Sam was wanted for seven felonies relating to drug dealing.

Instantly, Jesse knew the Junk House was noman's land. The gravity of such circumstances slowly dawned on him like effects of a poison pill dissolving on the stomach. Jesse reread the page to make sure this was authentic.

"So, they're looking for you now?"

"That's what it says."

"May I respectfully ask why the fuck are you sitting here right now? Besides the house, this will be the first place they look."

"I just got here."

"I wouldn't stay long. Disappear into thin air. Don't make it easy on them."

"It doesn't matter, Jesse."

"I think it does."

"Have I ever told you that you worry too much? You always have. Your soul's on the right side. Never worry."

"But a shit storm is coming down," Jesse insisted.

"Indeed it is," muttered Sam in a distant tone. Sam ordered another happy hour margarita. He lit a cigarette. Salt lingered in his untrimmed moustache.

"I suppose I do need to stay out of sight. I'm not going to jail."

"You need to leave town."

They watched ESPN Sports Center on the TV. Sam's Levi Garrett hat sat low on his head. He wore mirrored sunglasses and a red and white Hawaiian shirt. Jesse felt that his current home had become an evil funhouse. He reread the xeroxed page for the third time. The cryptic legal jargon directed at his favorite downtown friend created an outlandish element in his writer's mind. He wondered how deep the local sting operation penetrated. The digital clock read 4:47 p.m.

"Well, I better make like a baby and head out," said Sam as he grinned and put his right hand on Jesse's shoulder. They shook hands. Jesse searched for something proverbial to say, but amid the ominous legal complexity and circumstance of the moment they both decided to act like they would see each other the next day.

"Okay, Sam. Godspeed, my brother."

"Adios."

One final wave and Sam disappeared out the back door. Neither man understood it would be the last time they would ever see each other.

21

A week later Sully and Annie drove home from a friend's party on a humid, late June morning. Sully's subdued demeanor prompted Annie to talk.

"I'm really worried about Sam. He had a lot of powder. He needs to leave town."

"He said he's going to Mexico," Sully replied.

"He's known about the charges since yesterday."

Hours later, safe at home, after a few more drinks and lines of dust, they communicated in intoxicated waves of uninhibited, unrestrained and innuendo-filled dialogue. Annie was unable to hold her tongue. She was exhausting Sully's tolerance for her.

"Make me a drink," Annie told Sully as she chopped out more lines of powder. She wore Sully's cowboy hat. A tension smoldered in the room. Tonight Annie's tone proved confidentnearing belligerent. She knew something Sully didn't.

"Did you hear about Avalina?"

"No."

Sully placed the drink in front of her, and sniffed another line off the mirror.

"She ate a bottle of Valium."

Sully's stomach dropped. He wanted a cigarette, but he didn't want Annie to see his hands shaking.

"Are you making that up?" he asked.

"Why would I make it up?"

"Because sometimes your sense of humor sucks."

"She's not dead, but she tried to kill herself. I always knew that little bitch was crazy."

"That's classic coming from you."

"Are you insinuating that I'm crazy?"

"No, not you, you're not some deranged cunt who will say all kinds of evil bullshit."

"Hey! Fuck you! I didn't force those pills down her throat!"

"You might as well have."

Sully sat down and pulled out his cigarettes and lit one. He took a sip of his drink and stirred it with his pointer finger and without taking his eyes off Annie, said: "I want you to listen to this warning because I'm only going to say it once. You need to shut your godforsaken mouth and just give me the drugs."

She produced the bag of powder from her purse and tossed it to Sully. Picking the bag up off the floor, he opened it with great deliberation. She slid the mirror toward him.

"Our time together has run its course," Sully said solemnly.

Annie stood up and walked to the bathroom. A few minutes later Sully watched as she walked from the bathroom, through the living room, and out of the apartment without saying another word.

Jesse turned on the radio in his truck, and he was greeted with a news report of a 747 crashing into the Florida everglades killing all passengers on board. It was Saturday morning and he was leaving Sara's on the way to Sully's birthday party, thrown by Silvertone Jim Turner.

Driving along he noticed a dancing bear sticker on a Volkswagon. He already knew this was going to be a strange day. He drove several miles lost in the news reports of the plane crash when he thought he noticed Sam Tanner getting out of a car pulled off on the side of the interstate.

Another car pulled behind Sam. Sam looked like an undercover agent-late 30s, sunglasses, moustache and a ball cap pulled down over his longish hair. Jesse knew even at sixty-five milesperhour that it was Sam getting out of the car. He could recognize him from a mile away...the way Sam carried himself.

Jesse couldn't do anything but keep driving. He looked in his rearview mirror and saw that Sam was getting into the other car. Jesse wondered what was going on.

When Jesse told his friends at Sully's birthday party what he saw, they snickered at him as if he were a fool.

"Sam's in Mexico," said Sully with confidence.

"Slick, you have no idea what you're talking about," said Fleshman. He turned to Sully and said, "That guy is whacked. Where'd you find him again?"

Jesse held his tongue, feeling isolated from everyone in attendance. At one point in the evening, Jim Turner brought out some Rolling Stones CDs for Jesse, as a peace offering to keep him occupied. Everyone else partied in the entertainment room. It stung Jesse the way that Sully left him out in the cold.

Jesse had long been concerned about the ways Sully was swayed by his more famous and influential friends. Jesse became the odd man out. He needed Sara here. The change that Jesse knew he needed to embrace suddenly seemed more inviting and less painful to consider.

As Jesse walked away from the Stones CDs and back into the entertainment room, he overheard Sully say, "If Jesse is going to move out, I wish he'd get it over with already."

After hearing Sully, his conviction was unarguable.

He knew he had to leave town right away. Nothing felt the same.

...

Jesse spent the next week packing some books and albums to load for his move. As he neared the end of his first load, Sully came home and sat on the couch watching his activity. After a few minutes of silence between them, Sully spoke up.

"Jesse, remember you said you saw Sam on the side of the road? Turns out, it was really him. Jim Turner told me he's been hiding out in Atlanta with his ex-wife. I guess you were right all along."

It comforted Jesse to hear Sully revealing the facts and verifying his instincts, but it also further solidified the distance between them. Jesse noticed that Sully was becoming a little more self-absorbed in his recent local stardom. He was no longer acting like a brother to Jesse who had long championed his cause. Good musician. Shitty human being. Jesse thought this to himself while he remembered how his old actor friend, Red Florence, once referred to Sully as cliche.

After years of hearing his stray lines turn up in Sully's songs, Jesse felt for a moment like Sully merely stole the lines he wrote. However, Jesse knew deep down that wasn't true. Still, Sully seemed to encourage hacks to serve as literary wits these days. Or so it seemed to Jesse at this point. Time would tell.

Jesse smelled a neighbor's wood smoke burning as he stepped outside with a fresh cup of coffee and a pipe full of reefer to enjoy on Sara's back porch. Once he was high, he returned inside and sat down at the typewriter. He reached into his black rucksack and pulled out the small Black Cat medicine case, took a Percocet the Cook had given him and swallowed it.

For a few moments, he scanned the immediate items in front of him: a cup of coffee, a pipe, a 1995 *Farmer's Almanac*, a deck of cards, a sack of reefer, a burning cinnamon candle, a Flying Burrito Brothers compilation CD, Willie Nelson's *Shotgun Willie,* Coltrane's *Crescent,* Faulkner's short stories, Blind Willie McTell's *Atlanta 12 String,* a halfpint of Jim Beam, a book of Bob Dylan's lyrics, and Robert Frank's *The Americans.* As he stared at Sara's new Indian rug beneath the table, Jesse considered eating at a neighborhood barbecue shack tonight.

Sara left for work several hours ago. Jesse got up and opened the back door to aerate the lingering bacon scent from breakfast. He lit some incense. When he sat down again the phone rang. He thought it was Sara until he heard Jethro Monroe's voice.

"Jesse?"

"Hey. What's up?"

"Can you believe the news about your boy?"

"Who?"

"Sam Tanner."

"What about him?"

"I'm talking about finding him dead in Atlanta. Hell, all those that said he was in Mexico were way off."

"What? When did this happen?"

"They found him last night."

"Where?" Jesse asked as if it couldn't be true.

"Somebody's apartment. I heard the needle was still in his arm."

"Unbelievable," Jesse uttered in a voice that did not sound like his own.

"What timing. He doesn't have to go to jail now."

"This is bad news," Jesse said with a sullen acceptance.

"Sorry, I figured you already knew."

"No, this is the first I heard about it. Thanks for calling."

"Give me a call when you get back into town. It's been awhile."

"Ok, see you soon."

Jesse found Monroe's news difficult to comprehend. Sorrow descended on Jesse. He felt bad for Sam's wife and daughter.

...

After a few hours passed, Jesse called Sully to verify the news. Sully answered, half asleep, to confirm Sam died of an overdose, but he didn't mention where he died. Sully wasn't very conversational.

Jesse wanted to ask why he didn't call him to send the news, but he said nothing. Sully informed him the funeral was Tuesday. Jesse told Sully he'd see him then. The ruthless wheel of change ground forward. The sad news made him want to drink a beer.

He opened one of Sara's Heinekens and stared out the windows toward the rolling hills. Two crows stood on a bare limb peering into his window. It was a time of reckoning. Plans for the future were made on that morning, and they revolved around him and Sara.

By the late afternoon he already drank five beers. Staring at his typed pages, he couldn't get his mind off why Sully didn't call him with the news. He wondered about the unraveling threads of their friendship. He filled his pipe again, and remembered his good times with Sam.

24

A pariah walks on the outskirts of town gazing at a bloodred sunset. The evening sky seems to evoke some ominous warning. Here no lost idolaters loiter amid clockless hours of carnivalistic evil. Feeling one's own teeth rotting in the skull...out of money...out of vice... madness is never far behind...one of those days when the world feeds off misery and disaster.

Some lonesome train echoes through a fall evening. A full pink moon rises. This forsaken soul feels an immense darkness gathering within him like some biblical curse. Penumbras lurk within a riddle of eternal tribulation pondering the jinx of doubt. A desperate gravity pulled him toward a perilous unknown as if he were manipulated by some mysterious agent of evil. He stepped gently into his dark, transient dwelling, feeling an impending sense of spectacle.

25

The solemn drive back to town for Sam's funeral proved a symbolic trip for Jesse. The leaves changed colors. Distant wood smoke could be smelled through the slightly opened windows as he drove through the quiet rolling hills.

Endless days of the same routine were broken forever. At this moment, driving back to this scene, Jesse felt that his instincts served him well. He should never betray sheer insight. The closer he got to town, the more old memories reminded him of youthful days. Lack of a heater reminded him he needed a new truck. His tape player was broken, and he was tired of listening to the radio.

The atmosphere around the Junk House would now be nothing less than sinister to him. He'd never return. Jesse never liked the peripheral people around the House and the web they were caught up in. This would be his last drive back to town as a resident.

When Jesse arrived at the apartment, Monroe was coincidentally closing the front door as Jesse climbed the stairs.

"Hello, Jethro. Why don't you step back inside for a minute."

"Gladly. I came by to see if you were in town yet."

When Jesse shut the door, Jethro gave him a pat on the back and said, "I'm sorry about Sam. I know he always liked you, and y'all were tight."

"Yeah."

"What time is the funeral?"

"Two o'clock. Do you have anything on you?"

"I've got one gram left." They made an exchange.

"Thanks. When did you start buying this much to sell?"

"I just got a good deal."

"This will come in handy. I'm sure it's going to be a long, weird day."

"I bet. Call me when you can."

"Okay, man. Thanks."

Jesse felt better now that he scored. He heard Sully playing his guitar in his bedroom. He knocked and stuck his head in to say hello.

"What's happening?"

"Not much. Want to ride to the funeral with Annie and I?"

"Sure, hey I scored. You wanna do one?"

"I can't think of a better time." They shared disbelief of Sam's death in consolation of getting high in the other's company. They snorted a few sobering lines. Annie came after a bit and quietly joined in with them. They soon left to take the quiet ride out to the cemetery.

Today stood as one of the few days the chemistry between Sully, Annie and Jesse didn't feel negative. The dust elevated them, intensifying the gravity of this funeral. In his usual limited taste, Sully wore torn blue jeans, a red flannel shirt, tennis shoes, a red scarf and an old torn and frayed corduroy jacket. Annie wore a black sweater and dress. Amid the craziness, Annie appeared uncharacteristically subdued and unhostile.

A cold wind blew outside the funeral home. The locals embraced one another upon arrival. Jesse saw Jim Turner of the Silvertones shed tears. Years before, Sam supported many of these musicians before they could support themselves. Many only knew Sam as a local drug dealer. Jesse and others understood he was an instrumental character in the early days of this community of musicians and artists.

The three of them sat down in the back of the church. Many locals turned out for Sam's funeral. Various friends got up to speak, and Fleshman played the master of ceremonies. He borrowed two of Jesse's CDs Funkadelic's *Free Your Mind And Your Ass Will Follow* and Dylan's *John Wesley Harding*. Jesse thought these were strange selections, but he felt satisfied that Fleshman used something from his collection to play at the wake.

Sonja Lee, a girl Sam dated, sat in the pew directly in front of them and sobbed during the eulogy. Jesse didn't know all of the people, but Sam was his friend, and it was absolutely necessary for Jesse to pay his last respects.

Sam looked peaceful in the casket. Deep bruises existed below his eyes, and he seemed a shell of himself now that his spirit was gone. They dressed him in his favorite blue jeans, black Chuck Taylor tennis shoes, and an Allman Brothers tee-shirt. When they closed the casket, Jesse watched Fleshman and Lennear snort two lines off Sam's coffin. He considered it a bad omen for them.

Once the funeral ended, everyone drove downtown to the Marshall Hotel for a scheduled wake. Sully played a song with various musicians, including members of the Silvertones, in an impromptu session. The music, food and drinks uplifted all in attendance. Jesse felt a sense of camaraderie and peace.

Anticipating that people were about to leave, Fleshman instructed them all to move out on the deck for a group photograph. After that, Sully and Jesse began to separate from the crowd. They realized there was no longer a reason to stick around. They paid their respects, now all they could do like everyone else, was move on into the future, each carrying memories of Sam and the past.

Sully left Annie there with her friends while he and Jesse walked back to the apartment. They bonded in this strange and changing time as if death reminded them of their sacred brotherhood. This resembled an oldtime feeling just the two of them talking about music, books, films, getting high with no one else around.

When they got back home, they turned on the stereo and sat down to their indulgence feeling a rare light shining upon them. They understood soul outlasts flesh.

These brothers talked and laughed for a while rekindling the spirit of days past. In a brief moment, Jesse looked at his old friend's smile. Jesse saw teeth as a life symbol; decaying or clean, loose or rooted. Sully's smile revealed teeth in serious neglect.

"Man, I'm moving out next week for good. I'm gonna be with Sara," Jesse said to Sully.

"I had a feeling you were on the fade moving your books and music...you're not around much anymore," said Sully.

"This place makes no sense to me anymore. We're exiles on main street here."

"It's definitely not like it used to be."

"I'm not getting any writing done."

"I understand."

"I'll have everything out next week. It's the end of an era."

"Feels like it. Well, man, you know I love you."

"I wonder sometimes," Jesse said back with a short laugh.

"You never need to wonder, my brother."

From that moment on time condensed. Years flashed by in a moment. Yesterday is ash and memory. They began one of their rare heart-to-heart conversations that existed where the past, present and future converge. Flashes of telepathic communication arose between them like the days of old.

...

Caught in the euphoria of their circumstances, they decided to go back downtown. They were knocked out loaded, so they decided to call a taxi. When they walked into The Neon Eel, it was crowded by the remnants of Sam's funeral.

Jesse noticed two beautiful, drunk blonde girls kissing at the bar as he and Sully went to stand next to them. Jesse was buzzed enough to ask: "Will y'all kiss me like that?"

The blondes took turns kissing him and then moved on to Sully. They bought the boys shots of tequila.

"You're coming home with me," the blonde with blue eyes said to Jesse.

He relented to her wishes without resistance as his moral compass was clouded by hours of emotion, grief and inebriation. Jesse and Sully didn't have much time to talk after that. They lazily winked at each other as the blondes separated and corralled them.

The next morning, Jesse got his beauty, Vanessa, to take him home. She drove him in her silver BMW. She kissed him and dropped him off, and he prepared to drive back to the city to be with the girl he planned to marry. He stepped into another outpost of time...

Sam Tanner's death made turning on the Junk House gang easier for Felix Mendoza. He heard Fleshman took over Sam's distribution clientele. Felix felt no remorse in setting up Fleshman and anyone else connected to him.

Rosco Williams left Felix a sharp message, communicating urgency of an impending bust. Felix knew through Lennear where and when he and Fleshman were making a big score. Felix tried to discover where Cook scored his pills, but Lennear claimed The Cook never revealed his source. Felix confirmed to Williams that he would be present for the bust as they previously agreed.

The sight of the great Smoky Mountains refreshed Jesse's soul. The familiar Bryson City sign appeared by Highway 441 as he drove to his grandmother's house located a few miles up the road. Sara slept by his side. Childhood memories flooded his mind as he passed this road sign he'd not seen in years. Rain clouds hovered over the mountains in the mid October sky. Fall arrived. Through his barely opened window, a scent in the air reminded Jesse of his favorite Japanese incense. His family took this drive every summer and fall that he could remember.

In these mountains he planned to set the future into motion. It felt good to be far away from the downtown jackals.

This year, Jesse brought Sara along. His parents decided to visit as well. Jesse needed a new perspective. He hoped this trip would unlock old mysterious inspirations. Sara slept and Jesse didn't want to wake her until they arrived at his grandmother's house. He wanted their trip to the mountains to serve as an escape from common surroundings and routines.

For years, Jesse faced the same financial dilemma. The stakes rose each month. He knew the financial necessity of employment lingered. He wasn't a coat-and-tie man, but even if he tried to obtain a job at the local newspaper, he'd be forced to make lifestyle changes. Drug tests for one. He knew he had been in a pestilent phase for the last year or so. Previous careless days had come to an end. He'd have to make sacrifices to pursue his own life and art.

Jesse sipped herbal tea he had mixed before the trip. He wanted to purify his body from all the toxins he ingested these last days and months. He decided to focus all of his time on writing sober. He believed he had neglected his talent for too long.

He crept down Jefferson Branch Crossing through the dense forest on the way to his grandmother's. Old scars ached in this new era of life. A rite of passage descended.

He knew Sara wanted a family. He always feared raising children in this mean old world, which delayed the traditional process with Sara. They dated on and off for eight years, and everyone kept asking them the obvious question.

He loved her and understood she'd make a great wife and mother. She was smart and pretty. The fact that she didn't do drugs appealed to him in this new era. Every now and then she'd smoke with him, but she was subjected to random drug tests at work. She never indulged in narcotics.

Jesse considered all the love, turmoil and change he endured with this girl, and he had come too far to leave her behind. He needed a calm place to write. Things were always calmer around Sara.

Two miles from his grandmother's house-past the painted barns and roadside farmer's markets Jesse drove on, realizing his future with Sara hinged on his ability to make money. He drove transfixed by his solitary game of financial paradox. Yet, they knew each other long before money was an issue. Sara had been loyal and supportive and was even more so in this new era.

Overcast skies hovered over the steep roads. Jesse pulled out his small pipe that looked like a cigarette, and smoked a lungful of potent reefer. It smelled like the mountainous North Carolina terrain they drove through. He blew the illegal smoke out of the window. Sara didn't stir. He knew he'd have to cut back on this final vice.

No concrete, steel or asphalt surrounded him. Jesse found himself thinking back on his childhood friends that still live in these hills. They existed in his mind like ghosts. His literary pursuits had pushed him far past their conventions, conceptions and mundane perceptions. He harbored no illusions about returning to glory days of his childhood past. His was a solitary journey. These mountains provided a space and distance that allowed a clear perspective of his situation.

He cringed at running the gauntlet for employment. The painful road of progression waited ahead, but he would not allow his talent to play second fiddle. He brought his novels, articles and a few choice books with him on this trip to stay inspired.

He moved out of the apartment with Sully a month ago, and it already felt like a year. A drizzle of rain began to fall as he pulled into his grandmother's gravel driveway. He heard a lonesome train whistle blow in the distance.

Doreen served drinks to Fleshman, Lennear and Felix at The Neon Eel. The warm October weather cast a strange anticipation, or uneasiness, over this group since Sam usually handled such matters.

"Brokedown Palace" played over the bar speakers.

They recognized their fate remained beyond their control. They hid fears that the golden age was over.

Lately, Fleshman and Lennear ran dope out of the Junk House, but they also used The Neon Eel in some obscure defiance of Sam's death. As was tradition, the Cook stayed clear of any involvement with this current business. He'd gone beyond trying to convince his friends to follow his discreet path.

Without Sam things weren't the same around the Junk House. He had served as the nucleus for this gang that no longer seemed impenetrable. The magic vanished.

Felix built the foundation of his betrayal, and now everything fell into place. Through Rosco Williams, Felix gave Fleshman a fake buyer. Fleshman planned to sell two kilos of cocaine from Felix's source, who was supposedly driving in from Miami.

"So, this guy Frank, who's buying this shit is a friend of yours, right," Fleshman asked Felix.

"Yeah, after you score, we'll meet up with Frank."

"Something doesn't smell right. Why the hotel room?"

"He's from Miami. Unless you want him to stay at your place, what's the big deal? Sam always said you were paranoid."

"What time Friday?"

"3 p.m. Room 627 at the Holiday Inn on Broad Street."

December 31. Jesse returned from North Carolina almost three months ago. A week before Sully left him a message inviting him to a special New Year's Eve gig at The Black Rider Cafe. Jesse hadn't spoken to Sully since Sam's funeral.

Jesse noticed a gray hair in his beard as he looked in the rearview mirror while driving on 285 to Sully's gig. Sully was scheduled to perform with various local musicians tonight. Only one hundred tickets were available for this soldout show.

Jesse regretted leaving home for a scene he'd experienced so many times. As he drove on this familiar road, it surprised him when he felt the same sense of dread he experienced seeing Sam on the side of the road months ago.

A couple weeks ago Jethro Monroe called Jesse eager to talk about Sully. Jethro told Jesse that Sully kept a new crowd of people around him as of late. These new friends, that included roadies and managertypes, had Sully believing they could catapult Sully's career.

Jesse was familiar with many of the names Jethro gave him. He knew that these parasites were bold Silvertone's fans who were enamored by Sully's connection to that band. It was yet another example to Jesse of people driven by the alluring illusion of the rockandroll circus.

When Jesse arrived at The Black Rider Cafe after checking into his hotel room, he met several of these new sycophants. Most of these new "stage door Johnnies" ignored Jesse despite his tenure within Sully's inner circle.

Jesse noticed that Sully had hired a young guy named Spider as a new roadie. Spider was an old fan of the Silvertones. He stood six-foot one and one-hundred and weighed seventyfive pounds. He always wore a white shirt with a black skinny tie, black work gloves with the fingers cut off, a hat and flashlight on his belt.

Spider played drums in his own freeform band and considered himself quite the artiste. Spider even fancied himself a writer, and Jesse found humor in the idea that Spider might try to overshadow Jesse's literary stamp on Sully's musical lore. Jesse ignored, but detested, Spider's pushy countenance.

The Local Stranger

Jesse's arrival at the venue came after Sully's sound check. When Jesse walked past Spider, he found Sully drinking at the bar. They shook hands and Jesse sat down.

"Hello, my brother."

"How goes it?"

"Not too bad. Good to see you."

Jesse ordered a beer, and they once again fell into the chemistry of old. Sully removed his sunglasses and threw them on the bar.

"I guess you heard about the bust," Sully said lighting a cigarette.

"What bust?"

"It's been a couple of months ago."

"Nobody tells me anything."

"Fleshman and Lennear got busted with a couple of kilos at the Holiday Inn."

"First Sam. Now this. Smells..."

"Here may be the source of that smell. Felix was in the room, but as far as anyone can tell, he hasn't been charged with anything. Since then, he vanished. No one knows where he's at. In the meantime, I heard Lennear and Fleshman may get twenty-to-forty years. It's crazy."

"What about the Cook?"

"He moved out of the Junk House a month or so before the bust. Apparently he's not involved or implicated in any way."

"Heavy shit."

"I hate the idea of losing so many good friends."

Jesse didn't reply. He noticed that Sully looked rough. Even with the Junk House gang gone, these new vultures that surrounded Sully helped him very little. They walked toward the dressing room, and the new dealers seemingly appeared out of the shadows. Sully and his vultures disappeared into the dressing room with them.

Jesse did not partake in any contraband festivities and remained at the bar. He was leaving early in the morning. Jesse watched Sully's early set before midnight. He talked to a lot of friends, and enjoyed himself, but times had changed. After the show, as he walked across the street to his hotel, he knew that after all these years he'd been too much of a dove with such folks.

He didn't say goodbye to Sully. He'd see him soon enough.

In the hotel room, he took the phone off the hook as he sat on his bed and listened to fireworks explode.

~154~

The Second Word

I was struck from behind as I walked through a vulgar mob with a great weight upon my back. Multitudes of people formed a pathway that I followed. These men guarding me looked liked Roman soldiers.

When I focused, I realized they were beckoning me, prodding me in the back. "You're moving too slow!" they shouted, but I could only understand one solemn soldier that spoke.

My feet were bloody from tripping on rocks as I stumbled and lost my balance. People were spitting at me. The weight on my shoulders was overwhelming. Great splinters hung in my neck.

The faces of the people looking at me seemed solemn while others looked aggravated. Some hurled curses. It was chaos. The day was getting dark. Occasionally there was a whip brought down across my back. A stray rock crashed into my face.

The soldiers beat citizens slow to move out of the way. My mouth was dry and I fell to my knees. The weight on my back forced my face into the dirt. The crown of thorns wedged in the side of my head caused blood to flow down my face.

"Get up!" The soldiers and hecklers shouted as they kicked me in the ribs and pulled me up from the dirt by my hair. I was covered in spit and blood as they led me to the place of "The Skull." I was knocked down with great force by a sharp blow to the back of my head.

I fell down and gasped. I knew today was the day I must die as a whip snapped across my neck; I winced and rolled over on my back, staring at the darkening skies. I heard screams of my friend who had been convicted with me for stealing a Roman's bread.

The soldiers enjoyed when my friend screamed at them because they beat him harder. He was screaming "Fuck you," as they whipped him unmercifully. I watched them force him down on wooden stakes shaped like a cross, and suddenly they grabbed me and did the same thing. I heard one, then two quick hammerings followed by my friend's bloodfreezing screams.

There were six soldiers holding me down as I felt an excruciating pain from stakes being driven through my feet. I screamed when they drove the nails into my hands. I looked to both sides and each hand was nailed to a post. Crucified. As the soldiers raised the cross, an excruciating pain tore through my body as I could feel my shoulders dislocate from their sockets.

My friend was screaming and cursing at the top of his lungs. He was out of his mind. I could only remain silent as I felt my life slowing draining away. Below us the soldiers were slapping the Nazarene, whom I had heard speak in the city. He wore a crown of thorns and a purple robe. Blood ran down his face. He had been beaten and whipped, but I could not forget the intense gaze in his eyes. They were unearthly.

The crowd hurled insults at him and laughed as onlookers mocked him. Only the women were weeping. As they drove spikes through him, he gasped only a little. He did not speak or resist. The soldiers nailed a sign or something over his cross I could not read or see.

They hoisted the Nazarene upon a cross between my friend and me.

The crowd began shouting at him, "Save yourself, if you're the Son of God come down from the cross. Save yourself. You can save others, but you can't save yourself?"

The Nazarene quietly endured all the taunts with a serene dignity. I noticed two women standing together at the bottom of his cross. They were apparently his family. He seemed to speak to someone below him.

I wept at the sight of his suffering family. I had no family weeping for me. I had nothing. I was a thief being put to death for stealing a wealthy Roman's bread.

Some people rejoiced at the sight of the Nazarene being put to death. My friend was screaming to be taken down as he hurled blasphemies from his broken lungshe'd gone mad.

"Get us down from here if you are the One," my friend said to the Nazarene.

"Shut your mouth, Nicholas! This is our fate. Have you no fear of God? This man is being crucified with criminals, and he's innocent, so shut your mouth," I yelled at him.

I was tired. Color seemed to fade from my vision. It became more difficult to breathe, and my arms were separated from their sockets.

My mouth was dryer than cotton. The sky grew darker and the winds turned cold as people began running safely to their homes, while the soldiers divided the Nazarene's robe. One soldier stabbed him in the side with his spear. Another offered him a drink of vinegar.

I only wanted forgiveness. I wanted it all to be over. I was lonely. I asked the Nazarene if he would remember me when he was in paradise. He turned his head towards me. Blood ran down over his intense and revealing eyes, as if they looked through my soul, comforting me in their humility, and he uttered: "You shall be in paradise with me tonight."

I felt burning blood streaming from my mouth and heat from the spikes, but I could no longer breathe. A black muteness drowned out my senses.

I awoke clutching my chest, gasping for air, remembering the cryptic glance from the omnipotent eyes of the Nazarene only moments ago.

CPSIA information can be obtained
at www.ICGtesting.com
Printed in the USA
LVHW091805201022
731163LV00004B/542